YOU ARE THE
CLASSICS

FRANKENSTEIN

MARY SHELLEY
AND M. D. PAYNE

Penguin Workshop

Dedicated to the bold teen girl, Mary Shelley,
who broke down barriers to create history's
greatest monster—MDP

PENGUIN WORKSHOP
An imprint of Penguin Random House LLC, New York

First published in the United States of America by Penguin Workshop,
an imprint of Penguin Random House LLC, New York, 2021

Visit us online at penguinrandomhouse.com.

Library of Congress Cataloging-in-Publication Data is available.

Printed in the United States of America

ISBN 9780593095928

10 9 8 7 6 5 4 3 2 1 CW

Your carriage moves slowly along the well-worn path out of Switzerland into Germany. Your body shivers and bounces as the two horses struggle higher into the Alps. Your mind shivers and bounces as well—from thought to thought, from past to future. At the age of seventeen, you have left your home in Geneva for your studies at the University of Ingolstadt. You leave much behind, and your thoughts turn melancholy during the arduous journey. Then your spirits rise as you think about your future: a study of science that could affect the future of all mankind and tip the delicate balance of life and death toward life.

You have already made your own discoveries regarding life and its preservation without the assistance of scholastics. Part of you is afraid of where that might lead you if given even more resources and knowledge—and what you might become if you delve fully into that ghoulish science.

But what if you were able to unlock all the secrets of

death, so that none would ever suffer it again? You recently suffered such loss. Your dear mother was taken from you just months ago.

The rhythm of the carriage, the horses' hooves, and the crack of the driver's whip lulls you into a dreamlike state. You think of who you left behind in Geneva—your father; your older brother, Ernest; your younger brother, William; and your sweet Elizabeth, the gentle soul who first entered your home when you were both children. Her parents were too poor to take care of her, and so your parents took her in, to become your childhood companion. You call each other familiarly by the name of cousin. No word, no expression can describe the kind of relation in which she stands to you—since till death she is to be yours only. Once your studies end at the university, you shall marry Elizabeth.

The only glimmer of light that came of your mother's passing, the only thing that made you continue forward, was the sweetness Elizabeth showed you after your mother died. Never was she so enchanting as at this time, when she spent the sunshine of her smiles on you.

Everyone you love grows farther and farther from you as you journey toward your future. You, who have ever been surrounded by companions—you are now alone. You hoped your friend and confidant, Henry Clerval, could join you to study. Clerval tried to persuade his father to permit him to accompany you and become your fellow student, but in vain.

Your wandering thoughts are suddenly broken by a burst of light.

The carriage proceeds through a most violent and terrible thunderstorm. Thunder crashes with frightful loudness from every quarter of the heavens. You are suddenly filled with curiosity and delight, for you know the great power—the force of life—that can come from an electric shock. You press your face upon the window to get what view you can from the darkness outside, only to behold a stream of fire issue from an old and beautiful oak that stands just up the path.

Electricity's great power can also bring death in a flash.

The tree falls forward with an unearthly crash just as you pull your head back from the window and avoid the scratch of the branches that burst through.

The horses are not as lucky. They whinny a last frightened call as the tree falls upon them with a deafening thud.

You are thrown to the front of the cabin.

For a brief moment, you are enveloped in silence and darkness. All you can hear is the ringing of your ears. Then you make out the sound of a pounding rain above your pounding head, and stumble outside of the carriage into a black night lit only by flashes of lightning.

You call for your driver, Jean. He responds to say he is fine, but points to the fallen tree ahead. You make out the figures of your two carriage horses underneath a tangle of branches. The great tree, brought down by the ferocious storm, has crushed one. The other whinnies and bucks, desperate to get free of its reins.

"Whoa," calls Jean, as he slowly approaches the horse. "Whoa, easy." He calms it down, and then crouches down next to the fallen horse.

"Oh, he is gone, gone!" wails Jean into the thunder. You feel sad for Jean. The bond between horse and driver is strong, and Jean suffers greatly at its breaking.

For a moment, you wonder if you can work to bring the horse back to life. The tools you have brought along in the carriage are rudimentary—your skills more so!

No, now is not the right time, you think.

Suddenly, an idea crosses your mind. You smile, and the driving rain splashes against your mouth and pours down your chin. The hindquarters of the dead horse are untouched—fresh materials to study in your quest to gain knowledge! You must collect this superior sample at once. But Jean must not see you at your work.

You turn to your driver, clutching your shoulder as if in great pain.

"Jean," you grunt. "How far is the next village? I cannot bear the pain of a carriage ride—the bouncing and shivering shall bring me to ruin. I must wait here while you run ahead and fetch a physician."

Jean starts to protest, "But, Master—"

"Ugh," you say, wincing, and clutch your shoulder and roll your eyes. You are a wonderful actor.

"Yes," Jean says, recovering his composure. "I see you are hurt. I shall go ahead to Schwarzhaus, an inn only a few kilometers from here. They shall know where to find a physician. Can I help you back into the car—"

"No!" you snap, not allowing him to look at your perfectly functional shoulder. "Do not waste time on me. I shall manage to get myself into the carriage and await your return. I must rest now. Go!"

You hobble over to the carriage and hoist yourself inside. Jean pushes past the tree on the path and quickly disappears from your sight.

"Do not turn around!" you hiss at him through the rain and jump out to unpack your large bags of equipment lashed to the rear of the carriage.

By the time you ready your tools and unhitch the dead horse from the carriage, the rain has stopped, and the moon begins to shine between wispy clouds. Another stroke of luck! You have all the light you need to do your work.

You approach the dead horse and feel its back leg. Still warm. The front of the beast is crushed grotesquely under the tree. Blood flows out from under the body. You grit your teeth and manage to saw the poor creature's leg off.

You stand up, gasping for air, and look down at your hands, covered in gore. Suddenly the moon seems too bright. You know what another might see if they came down the path at that very moment. A madman, a destroyer of flesh, a devil! You must clean up your work swiftly.

You take the leg and gently wrap it in cloth. It is large, but so are the cases that hold your instruments. You are able to fit it in. You use a puddle of rainwater to clean the blood from your hands and then quickly change your clothes. You cut a few branches off of the fallen tree to hide the missing leg.

But before you can, the horse that survived the tree stomps and whinnies. A figure pushes through the branches on the path and runs toward you.

Jean! Back so soon! The moon is now partially shrouded in clouds, but if Jean looks close enough, he shall most certainly see that someone has mangled his fallen horse. You don't have time to hide the missing leg, so you stand in front of the horses with the hope that Jean regards you when he arrives and not his legless horse.

You are so caught up in trying to figure out how to get him to leave, you forget to clutch your shoulder.

"There is something up the path," Jean states, "that we should tend to before we continue on to the inn. The way is smooth, and I shall drive slowly and . . ."

Before you can ask what is up the path, Jean looks at you strangely.

"What are you looking at?" you ask, terrified his eyes have caught the gruesome scene behind you.

"Your shoulder," Jean says, pointing. "You were in so much pain before . . ."

You are filled with a great relief!

"Oh, I must have been in shock because of the terrible crash," you quickly say. "Yes, indeed, now that the rain has ended, why, I feel rejuvenated. Let us proceed."

You breathe easier as Jean, now distracted by whatever lays ahead, quickly untangles his horse from the tree branches, modifies his equipment for one horse, clears the path ahead, grabs the reins, and jumps onto the driver's seat. You return to the carriage. There is a slight buck and a "WHOA" from Jean before the carriage moves once again.

Now in the privacy of your carriage, with no prying eyes to see, you smile so broadly as to bring pain to your cheeks. Jean did not notice his legless horse, and that leg, from such a freshly dead specimen, shall allow you to learn much about death, life, and the connection between the two.

Your spirits and hopes rise. It is time to look ahead—ahead to your future at the university. You ardently desire the acquisition of knowledge. You wish to reveal the secrets of nature. Wealth is not important, but how glorious it would be if you could banish disease and make man invulnerable to any but a violent death.

Just as you begin to feel comfortable that you shall make it to the university with enough time for your specimen to remain fresh, your carriage comes quickly to a stop. The horse whinnies loudly. Something upon the path must have frightened it. *What is on the path that Jean has stopped for?* you think, suddenly remembering what he said.

You exit the carriage in great annoyance. It is of the utmost importance that you reach the university and begin work on your new specimen at once. There is no time to waste, lest the flesh begin to decay.

You rush to the front of the carriage to admonish Jean, but run into a figure that emerges from around the front of the carriage at the same time. The figure, wrapped in a cloak to protect itself against the cold Alpine air, grunts as it hits the ground, facedown.

From under the folds of the cloak, you hear, "Please, sir. Help me."

You reach down to lift the person up and are soon regarding the most abhorrent face you can imagine. The mouth is filled with rotting teeth, and moldy gums where more teeth should be. The skin is terribly scarred and burned. You are immediately disgusted by this person. You know not if it is a man or a woman. The wiry long gray hairs that protrude from under the hood of the cloak give no clue. You feel you are face-to-face with a monster.

The monstrous person, noticing your expression, says, "Yes, sir, I do know that life has not been kind to me. Please do not amplify the effect by being cruel to me as well."

You turn to the driver. "You stopped us for this?" you ask.

"Master?" the driver says, shocked at your cruelty. "The air is thin and the night grows cold after the rain. Clearly this poor soul could use our help."

"Bah, Jean!" you say. "Though you drive it, this is my carriage, and I shall decide who we stop for, and when!"

You, too, are shocked by your cruelty. But you cannot help it. You can almost hear the bells tolling at the university, calling the goodly students to their lessons. You return to your carriage, step inside, and slam the door.

The wayward traveler looks at you through your broken window.

"Shall you really not help me, then, good sir?" asks the traveler. You can barely look at them as you contemplate your reply. They clasp their hands together as if in prayer.

You stare at the monstrous figure before you for some time. Your driver breaks the silence.

"Master Frankenstein?" he asks. "What say you? I shall obey your wish."

**If you decide to continue on
as planned, without helping the person,**
turn to page 111

**If you decide to help, and allow the person
into your carriage,** turn to page 130

*T*he French close in.

You must give up. You have lost control of your monster army. You lay down your tools.

"Master, no!" Igor screams above the din of battle.

But you have made up your mind.

"Igor!" you insist. "Flee!! Leave this place. This is my design, and it is only I who should be destroyed because of it."

A French bayonet slices between you and Igor. You deflect it long enough that he may escape the battlefield.

"Run!" you cry.

You grab the bayonet and turn it on the soldier who has approached you. You attempt to fight your way off the battlefield, hoping perhaps that you too can escape—and by some miracle evade the wrath of von Hindenburg after he retreats.

But, as you have ceased your efforts, the French have

now overrun your monster army.

The ones that remain, knowing that you are their creator, their father, fight with great determination to save you. In doing so, they are themselves destroyed. You are captured by the French and taken away from the carnage of the battlefield. You stand trial and are convicted.

Your head rolls after your trip to the guillotine.

THE END

You say not a word and convince yourself that Justine shall be acquitted.

You and your father are soon joined by Elizabeth. She welcomes you with the greatest affection. "Your arrival, my dear cousin," says she, "fills me with hope. You perhaps will find some means to prove my poor Justine innocent. If she is condemned, I shall never more know joy."

"She is innocent, my Elizabeth," say you, "and that shall be proved; fear nothing, but let your spirits be cheered by the assurance of her acquittal."

However, at Justine's trial, several strange facts combine against her. Horror fills the court when a locket is produced that was found in Justine's pocket; the same which, an hour before William was missed, Elizabeth placed round his neck.

You are there to witness, and you quickly see that the acquittal of which you were so assured is not a guarantee.

She is found guilty! You and Elizabeth attempt to move the judges from their settled conviction. Your passionate appeals are lost upon them. Justine perishes on the scaffold as a murderess!

You are trapped in a horror of your own making. Elizabeth, whom you love more than all, tries to help you.

"Dear Victor," she sweetly intones, "banish these dark passions. While we love, while we are true to each other, here in this land of peace and beauty, we may reap every tranquil blessing—what can disturb our peace?"

But not even the angelic Elizabeth can pull you out of your deep despair. You grow restless and seek the solace of nature. You venture into the Alps and attempt to soften your heart and calm your mind.

First on horseback, and then with a mule, you traverse beautiful valleys with rushing streams, the mighty Alps all around you. After reaching the village of Chamounix, you determine to ascend the imposing Montanvert to see the glacier from its summit.

As you admire the beauty of the glacier, you suddenly behold the figure of a man, at some distance, advancing toward you with superhuman speed. He bounds over the crevices in the ice, among which you had walked with caution; his stature, also, as he approaches, seems to exceed that of man. You perceive, as the shape comes nearer, that it is the unearthly, ugly wretch whom you created.

"Devil," you exclaim, "do you dare approach me? And do not you fear my fierce vengeance? Begone, vile insect! Abhorred monster! Fiend that you are! The tortures of hell are too mild a vengeance for your crimes. You reproach me with your creation; come on, then, that I may extinguish the spark which I so mistakenly bestowed."

"Be calm!" he says. "I am your creature, and I will bow to my natural lord and king if you will also perform your part. I ought to be your Adam, but I am rather the fallen angel, whom you drive from joy for no misdeed. I was good; misery made me a fiend. Make me happy, and I shall again be good. Listen to me, Frankenstein, and then, if you can, and if you will, destroy the work of your hands. Hear my tale; it is long and strange . . ."

If you listen to what the monster has to say, turn to page 168

If you throw yourself at him in vengeance, turn to page 55

"**N**o! I must not continue this unholy work," you say to von Hindenburg. "I have already gone too far. Your appearance before me today—your question—has made me resolute. I must not continue."

"Very well," says von Hindenburg slowly, watching to see if you change your mind. "But I am a man of my word, Mr. Frankenstein." He rattles the gate, and a foot soldier appears to open it.

"See to it that Mr. Frankenstein's . . . friend . . . is released at once," says von Hindenburg, and the foot soldier quickly turns and runs off to do the deed. Your heart sinks, but you know you have made the right decision.

Von Hindenburg turns back to you and presents you with a small card. He says, "You may soon regret your decision. If you do, I hope that I—and my proposal—remain in your mind. You may find me at this location."

He turns and leaves, his foot soldiers quickly following

behind him. A rush of fear courses through your body. You have created something that has already killed, has already wounded. For all you know, the wretch has already been released to seek revenge for your abandoning him and heads for you now.

You walk into the streets, pacing them with quick steps. You fear every turning of the street will present the wretch to your view. You feel a need to hurry on, although drenched by the rain, which pours from a black and comfortless sky. You pause at an inn. You do not know why, but you remain some minutes with your eyes fixed on a carriage that is coming toward you. It stops just where you are standing, and when the door opens, you see Henry Clerval, who, upon seeing you, instantly springs out.

"My dear Frankenstein," exclaims he, "how glad I am to see you! How fortunate that you should be here at the very moment of my arrival."

Nothing can equal your delight upon seeing Clerval; his presence brings back to your thoughts your father, Elizabeth, and all those scenes of home so dear to you. You grasp his hand and in a moment forget your horror and misfortune; you feel suddenly, and for the first time during many months, calm and serene joy.

Of all the souls on God's earth, it is Clerval to whom you tell all of your secrets, all of your dreams, all of your ambitions. Should you tell him of the nightmare that has transpired since you last saw his amiable form? Can you bear to have the truth out? A great relief could indeed be found. But what shall Clerval do if you reveal your secret?

If you tell Clerval about your creation, turn to page 99

If you keep quiet about all that has happened, turn to page 158

es. If you are to undertake such a task, you should not have to undertake it alone. You approach Elizabeth and confide in her everything that has occurred to you, and what you intend to do in order for the monster to relent.

As you lay out your tale, you regard Elizabeth closely to see how she reacts. At first, she appears shocked; her face whitens and fills with anguish and horror.

By the end, her face has softened, and you realize, without hearing her speak, that she shall not condemn you.

"Oh, dear Victor," she says, "what torture you have put yourself through! I am so glad that you have confided in me. Of course I shall seek to help you. I intend to do everything in my power to create a companion for your creature that will bring him, and us, great joy."

You marry immediately and tell your father that you shall take an extended holiday in England. In reality, you intend to seek advice from noted British scientists in order to improve your knowledge. After a few days of leisure, you arise one morning to tell Elizabeth that you are off to listen to the learned men of Oxford University.

"I shall accompany you," says she.

"Elizabeth, the university is no place for a woman."

"Victor, if your intent is for me to aid you, I require the same tutelage. There is no arguing on this point."

You are shocked, and yet, knowing she is still willing to help you despite your terrible crime, you relent.

She soon becomes an astute student of science. Not only does she assist you, she leads you in fresh new directions, suggests modifications that would have never occurred to you had you labored alone.

You move your laboratory to a remote hut on a dreary Scottish island, so that no prying eyes may witness your work—save for the eyes of your creation. You do not doubt that he monitors your progress and will visit you when the time is come to receive his bride.

You are proud of Elizabeth, and your work continues along swiftly. Yet, as you continue with this work, a deep horror creeps into you.

You have brought Elizabeth into the dark land where only you before had traveled. You have sullied such a beautiful creature in order to create such an ugly one. You suddenly realize that none of this may continue. For you, and now she, have conspired to create another demon to unleash upon the world.

One moonlit evening, as the figure which lays before you upon the table appears particularly disturbing, you cannot remain silent anymore.

"Elizabeth, I am eternally grateful for all you have done to bring me this far—"

"To bring *us* this far," she says.

"Yes. But what we regard as progress may very well be a regression against nature! Who are we to create such a creature? Who was I to create such a creature before? In their union, will they not be more damnable and terrifying? We would do well to cease our labors."

"Dear cousin, I have heard your tales. I know your mistake. It was that you abandoned your creation and did not foster it. In creating this bride, you are indeed providing your creation with what he needs."

"And what of her?" You point at the lifeless figure on the slab. "She comes from nothing and knows nothing. Will she not be of an evil nature similar to him?"

"Oh, cousin, do you not listen to me? Of course she shall not, just as we shall not abandon her. We shall assure that she and he are given everything they need to live in peace and harmony. Perhaps even one day to become part of society . . ."

You are perplexed. You have the deepest trust in

Elizabeth. And yet, you have only relayed the horrors you experienced with your first creation—she has not seen them firsthand.

What is the proper course of action?

If you decide to destroy what you have made together, turn to page 34

If you listen to Elizabeth, turn to page 73

When your eyes are not on your work, they are locked onto the dull, yellow eyes of the demon.

After the final stitch, and just before you jolt the still pile of flesh into life, you say, "I have your word, then? You shall leave humanity alone?"

The monster nods. He climbs through the window and motions you to proceed.

As if in a nightmare, the bride rises. She struggles a moment to balance her massive frame and walks toward your creation. As scarred and horrific as she is, he lovingly embraces her and whispers soothing words. He knows what it is like to be born in such a way. For a moment, you pity both of them. If only you had embraced your creation in such a way when he was born, perhaps you would not find yourself here now. The monster and his new companion leave you.

You fall into a deep slumber, caring not if you have made

the right decision. When you wake, you determine to exile yourself. You do not deserve an angel such as Elizabeth. And you cannot bear to look your father in the eye.

Days later, you are still in a stupor. Henry Clerval arrives, but you barely recognize him. You had resigned yourself to the fact that you would wither and die at this place, and once again Clerval comes to the rescue.

"Dear God, Frankenstein," Clerval exclaims. "What on earth has happened? You asked for privacy, but I would have come sooner if I had—"

You cut your friend off. "Dear Henry, I did indeed ask for privacy. And privacy is still what I require. Please, you must make no inquiries as to why, but you must take on a task that shall pain your heart and mine."

You tell your friend that he must make your intention known to your family—you shall spend the remainder of your days on this barren island. You have seen loathsome things in humanity and yourself that you cannot unsee, which you can never share. Your heart and soul are ruined, and you dare not return to them lest they develop the same malaise by seeing it in one they love. They must forget you.

You know that your father can offer you a stipend from which to live meagerly. You beg Henry to explain all of this to your family and secure the stipend from your father.

Clerval agrees.

You spend your years on the island alone, a hermit

surrounded by nothing but the winds and rains. You age terribly, and find yourself near death a mere ten years after Henry leaves. You send him a message, and barely cling to life when he appears once again at your door four weeks later. He still looks young—in the prime of his life—while you have withered away.

"Clerval," you croak. "Tell me of my father, and of Elizabeth. Are they well?"

"Both are well," Henry says.

"I am so glad," you say and begin to feel the life fade away from you.

Henry gives you a strange look.

"Fear not, Henry," you say. "Death is only natural. I just needed to hear that all was well. You have done so much for me. I have been such a burden in your life, but you have carried me, and for that I will sing your praises in the heavens—if I am lucky enough to ascend there."

Still Henry looks bothered.

"What is it?" you ask.

"Oh, nothing," says he. "I wish not to disturb you with such trivial things."

"Go on, friend," you say. "Tell me a story to put me to sleep."

"In truth," says he, "I am deeply distracted from what I have heard on my way here. Apparently, strange 'big people' have been sighted on an island nearby. There are monstrous little children running around naked in the cold, and the chill seems not to have any effect."

A lump forms in your throat. You cannot believe what you hear. The wretch and his bride had children!? And remained so close to you! Why? To taunt you? You cough fitfully and try to reach for a breath to ask hundreds of questions of Clerval.

"There, there," says Clerval, "I meant not to bother you with such superstition in your final moments. Come, let us speak of other things."

But it is too late. The news has made your very heart stop.

You die.

THE END

"**H**err Kapitän," you say to von Hindenburg, "with all due respect, I prefer to work alone. And even if I was in need of assistance, I certainly would not turn to this . . . heathen."

"Oh." Von Hindenburg raises an eyebrow. "I merely wished to make sure you have everything you need so that you could assure I have everything *I* need. But if you are determined you can manage on your own . . ."

Von Hindenburg turns to the soldier. "Release him."

Igor does not hesitate. He flees, laughing wildly like a madman. When Igor is fifty feet away, von Hindenburg motions to his soldier once again. The soldier gives von Hindenburg his rifle.

Igor is now sixty feet away. His laughter has changed to cheering. Von Hindenburg raises the rifle. Still, Igor runs. Seventy feet . . . eighty feet . . . Von Hindenburg fires. Igor falls.

"Danke," says von Hindenburg, and he hands the rifle back to the soldier. The soldier salutes and leaves. You crane your neck until it pains you to see what has become of Igor.

"I assure you, Herr Doktor," says von Hindenburg, "your former assistant is very much dead. I rarely miss. A good lesson for you to learn, yes? Do you now understand what will happen to you if you run?"

You say yes, but you do not even hear yourself. You sway in place, overcome by fear, suddenly wishing you had help—any help—to assure you can provide von Hindenburg with what he desires.

"Good, then!" he says, grinning ear to ear. "Let me take you to your laboratory, as it were."

He leads you to a charnel house on the outskirts of the camp. You are shocked by the amount of bodies, piled high. Behind the bodies are instruments the likes of which you have never dreamed.

Von Hindenburg sees the smile form on your face.

"I can tell you like what you see," he says. "Go on, then! Get to work! I expect one hundred new soldiers in a fortnight, when we head once again to the front lines."

You panic. You were only able to make one monster after months of study and labor. How can you make one hundred in just a fraction of the time?

Before you can protest, von Hindenburg is gone.

Your efforts are a disaster from the start. You barely

have time to sew and bring anything to life, so busy are you with the onerous task of moving bodies around.

You have been sent upon a fool's errand, and indeed there is little chance you may create more than three or four soldiers in the time ordered by von Hindenburg. In times of stress and worry such as this, you have ever relied upon the counsel of your dear cousin, Elizabeth, to work out what you should do next.

Elizabeth! Oh, dear Elizabeth. You ache to see her now, but begin to think that no matter what transpires on this wretched battlefield, you may never see her again.

If only you could send her a letter, perhaps she could help you leave this damnable place?

But you are unsure. *Oh no!* you think. *Involve Elizabeth not! She is safe, bring her not into harm's way.*

What should you do?

If you send Elizabeth a letter,
turn to page 58

If you decide to leave her out of it,
turn to page 146

No, you've come this far, and you have every intention of continuing your work. Your aim is not to create a mindless bag of bones, but a new human being. And humans do not just come, their first day on earth, equipped with everything they need. A human can only think for itself after years of training from its parents. You have finished the body. Now you must work on its mind. You must raise this "child."

You grab the outstretched appendage of your creation, and wince when you feel it is still cold. You fight back the bile that rises in your throat when you remember how many graves you have robbed just to put this arm together. With teeth clenched in disgust, you carefully pull your creation to your breast like a mother would a child.

The thing trembles in your arms. He still reeks of the grave. You hum to calm him, and to calm yourself. Finally, resolved to follow through on your decision, you speak softly to him.

"Welcome," you say. "Welcome, my friend."

Upon hearing your voice, his body becomes tense. He lets out a low moan, the sound of a creature filled with doubts.

"Yes, I know," you say. You continue to soothe him as a mother would her baby. "It is all so very confusing, but you are here now." You hold him a little bit tighter, but the creature breaks loose, perturbed by your affection.

"Wait, wait," you say, still in a soft voice. "I am here to help you." You hold up your arms, but the creature is confused. He stumbles back and away from you, bumping into the dresser where you keep your clothes. The mirror on top of the dresser tumbles off and shatters with a loud sound that disturbs your creation. He throws his hands over his ears and crumples onto the floor.

You approach him slowly, worried that you might drive him off—or worse, cause his fear to transform into an uncontrollable rage. You brush away the shattered mirror and sit down next to him, putting your hands over his hands, which still clutch his ears, desperate to block out any sounds that might disturb him.

You cannot force his hands off of his ears, and you dare not speak with him, so you resolve to hold him silently for as long as it requires to calm him. His body shakes. Countless minutes pass, until finally, he removes his hands from his ears. You still think it wise not to speak, but you pat his black mat of hair, drenched with sweat from the anxiety he feels at being in this new world. You stroke him gently, feeling where your stitchwork runs underneath.

He whimpers, but gives no indication that he will once again try to flee. Slowly, he lowers his head onto your lap. The great snores soon emanating from his bulk reveal that he is indeed sleeping.

You and he sleep fitfully on the floor through the night. Each time he awakens, you calm him. You say soothing things into his ears. You tell him you are his friend. You tell him not to worry.

By morning's light, the creature has calmed to the point of making happy sounds. You sit him at your breakfast table and attempt to feed him. It is just as he breaks his fourth plate of scrambled eggs that a knock comes at the door.

Both you and your creation freeze in place, unsure of how to react to the sound.

"Who is it?" you say loudly but calmly.

"Frankenstein, let me enter!" says a familiar voice. "It is I, Henry Clerval, here to become a learned man!!"

Good God, Henry Clerval! You know not if his timing is perfect, or terrible.

Your creature lets out a low moan and grips the table. He is worried about what is behind that door. Perhaps he thought you and he were the only people in the world. Maybe you should let him think that for now . . .

Do you dare let Clerval in?

Or, rather, should you ignore him so that you can focus on your work of bettering this newly formed beast?

If you remain silent,
turn to page 65

If you let Clerval in,
turn to page 49

"**N**ay," you say. "I have started this terrible work, and it is *I* who shall determine when it is finished. We cannot continue."

Trembling with passion, you tear the monster's wicked bride to pieces.

"Victor, no!" Elizabeth screams. She points at the window. The disfigured form of he whom you detest most looks on in shock. His face disappears but for a moment, and then he bursts through the door and bellows, "You have destroyed the work which you began! Do you dare to break your promise? Do you dare destroy my hopes?"

"Be gone! I do break my promise; never will we create another like yourself, equal in deformity and wickedness."

"Please, dear soul," Elizabeth pleads with the demon. "He knows not what he does. I shall not deny you. Let me finish this work and counsel you on a bright future."

The monster points a crooked finger at Elizabeth.

"Man, you have condemned me doubly by having your companion support you in the way you know I need to be loved and supported, and then still bringing your endeavors to ruin. Were it not that it brought you so much joy, I would let her live. There are too few of her in the world. But now all whom you love shall die, so that you may languish in such a meager existence as I."

"Fiend!" you cry, and dash at him with a galvanizing tool. You set it to maximum power. The tip crackles with lightning-like sparks.

He grasps the tool before it can strike him and throws you to the ground. He jams the tool into Elizabeth, who is electrified so quickly she cannot even scream. She falls to the ground, dead and smoking.

The monster leers over her smoking body and laughs coldly. Reveling in his revenge, he notices not that you have a syringe in your hand, filled with poison. You approach him and empty it into his arm. He screams in great anguish.

"Now you shall die," you say.

"Frankenstein, we shall die together!" With a great howl he crushes your skull before the poison takes effect, and you fall together in a heap—creator and creation taken from the realm together, with nobody but the seagulls to witness.

THE END

"*I* beg of you, friend, step aside," you say to Clerval. "I must undo my unholy work. A thing of evil! His very existence makes me suffer."

You raise your arm over Clerval, but the wretch is aware of your intent. With great strength, he grabs your tool and brings it down upon the head of your friend. The last look you see on the face of your dearest companion is pity for the very creature that has destroyed him.

"No, Victor . . . ," gasps Clerval. "No . . ." His last words.

The monster pushes Henry's body upon you, and you collapse to the ground. He turns to leave. With great effort, you push Henry's body off of you and scream after the wretch, "No, come back! Finish what you have started. Kill me, for now I cannot live."

But your creation escapes into the night to leave you in ruin. A fitting punishment, for you shall be more miserable alive than dead. You fall upon Clerval's body in exhaustion, and sleep for some time. When you awake, you marvel that you have been left alone at the scene of such a grisly crime.

You know not what to do. You weep over your friend. Suddenly, you realize that there may be hope. Kapitän von Hindenburg could help you. Yes, von Hindenburg! With von Hindenburg, you could have your revenge.

Still, you hesitate . . .

You created one monster only to go mad and see your closest friend perish. What havoc would be wreaked upon the world if you created a whole army of monsters?

Should you resign yourself to your fate and hide from your one creation?

If you reach out to Kapitän von Hindenburg, turn to page 142

If you decide to go into hiding and live what life you can, turn to page 83

*T*he diminutive dogs you have collected provide you little to work with, though you take solace in the fact that whatever you create will be so small that it could never perpetrate any violence upon you with its tiny mouth filled with miniscule teeth.

You are relieved, too, that the construction does not take long. By the end of your third night, you have a perfectly viable specimen.

The wag of the tail signals that your creation has indeed come to life. You grasp its small form in your hands and feel life pulse through it. The creature shudders and shakes as if to escape you, but you hold it tight. It takes you a few days to train, and as you do, you notice the physical imperfections in your work. It has a limp in its right rear leg.

Soon, it becomes your companion, and for a time, you forget that this little mongrel was created by your hand.

Rather, you enjoy being with it, feeding it, talking with it, and walking it.

You do not hesitate to leave the university in the midst of instruction so that you may walk it. "I have to tend to an experiment," you say as you jovially exit. Your fellow students remark on how happy you seem to be.

It is during one of these walks in the middle of the day that you encounter a cat. The cat, sensing that something is different about this dog, raises its hackles. Your dog begins to whimper and pull at its leash. You do your best to reassure and calm your creation, but it is clearly terrified.

The cat continues creating a racket on the cobblestone road ahead of you, so you cautiously back down the way you came. Still the cat follows. Your dog, nearly electrified with fear, tugs ferociously on its leash until it escapes its collar! It runs away from the cat. You try to stop the cat from following, but it has other ideas—it slips right between your legs and catches up with your dog in no time, grabbing it by the throat.

A choked cry rises into the air. You rush to help your dog, but it is too late. Its small frame has already been torn asunder by the vicious feline. The cat looks at you while licking lips stained crimson, and then casually trots away. You crouch over your dog, and a wave of sadness trickles through your body. You wonder how you could have created something so unnatural—a dog that could so easily be destroyed by a cat.

For days and sleepless nights, you lament the loss of the dog, and curse your hands for creating such a helpless creature. You must do better!

You have hitherto hesitated to create a human after seeing such a wretched being as Karolina shunned by mankind, but you have learned much from your animals. You are sure you can make a human passable by society.

Yes, you must create a man!

Turn to page 70

As the weeks go by, you deeply cherish the time you spend with your childhood friend, Clerval. Together, you make great headway with the creature, and he begins to say words such as *no, yes,* and *hungry.* Soon after, he masters sentences.

You use what you learn at the university each day about anatomy, chemistry, and physiology to better the monster with small surgeries that assist his speech even further, make him steady enough to take care of himself, and make his appearance less horrific. You will never be able to make him perfect. There will still always be scar tissue, and deep gouges in the flesh where the stitches must remain. However, your creation has progressed by leaps and bounds both physically and mentally.

Unfortunately, so occupied are you with your work, that you notice not that your creation is beginning to wear on Clerval. After your creation falls asleep late one night,

Clerval comes to speak with you.

"Frankenstein," Clerval moans. "I cannot take much more of this! My whole life revolves around him—and around YOU! You bark orders at me all day, if you talk to me at all. And he follows me around incessantly."

"Clerval, you are doing wonderfully!" you assure your friend. "My experiment is doing so well. Yes, the labor is hard, but it will soon bear fruit!"

"I am at my wit's end, Frankenstein," continues Clerval. "You may not need sleep, but I do—and he sleeps not. I am up all hours of the night with him. You must take on more of his behavioral modifications with me!"

"I have not the time," you reply, "for I am solely focused on his anatomical functioning and language skills. I fear I would not be able to better his attitude without you. I fear we are both subject to the same detriment in our personality—I, too, have not the patience."

"Is it time then to call upon some other members of the student body or faculty of the university?" asks Clerval. "Perhaps they would be able to achieve greatness where we have failed."

"First, my dear Clerval, you have not failed," you say. "You have done so much for him. But he is not quite ready to be introduced to the greater scientific community. I am not sure who, at this point, could help us."

Henry is clearly at his wit's end. Who you need is

someone with great patience, someone who would be able to understand what your creature is going through and help him through it all. *Could it be me?* you think.

True, you could do your best to shift your focus to his mental needs, rather than his physical. It may be, in fact, that you could have more impact than Henry.

Still, as you knew from the start, Clerval is irreplaceable. And he has lifted your spirits as well. There is no one else on earth as good at doing that . . . except for Elizabeth!

Do you ask for her help?

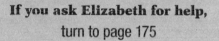

If you take care of the creature on your own, turn to page 81

If you ask Elizabeth for help, turn to page 175

You convince Elizabeth to go to bed.

She leaves you, and you inspect every corner of the house. But you discover no trace of him. Just as you determine all is well, you hear a shrill and dreadful scream. It comes from the bedroom. As you hear it, the whole truth rushes into your mind; you can feel the blood trickling in your veins and tingling in the extremities of your limbs. The scream is repeated, and you rush into the room.

Elizabeth is there, lifeless and unmoving, thrown across the bed, her head hanging down and her pale and distorted features half covered by her hair. Everywhere you turn you see the same figure—her bloodless arms and relaxed body flung by the murderer onto the bed. You fall senseless onto the floor.

When you recover, you see at the open window a figure most hideous and abhorred. A grin is on the face of the monster; he seems to jeer, as with his fiendish finger, he points toward the corpse of your wife. You fire your pistol, but he eludes you, leaps from the window, and, running with the swiftness of lightning, plunges into the lake.

You attempt to track down the monster, but in vain. You lose him in the wilds near the inn and are forced to return to Geneva without having captured your prey. A great guilt burns your soul, but you dare not reveal your secret—that it was *you* who created the beast that killed your dearest wife.

Your father, whose health had already declined during your time at Ingolstadt, falls deathly ill upon hearing the news of Elizabeth's brutal end. He cannot live under the horrors that have accumulated around him; he is unable to rise from his bed, and in a few days, he dies in your arms.

For some time, you know not what to do, and wander aimlessly around Geneva. One night, you find yourself in front of the family tomb—the crypt where those you loved so generously and who loved you so generously in return make their eternal repose.

You kneel on the grass and kiss the earth and with quivering lips exclaim, "By the sacred earth on which I kneel, I swear to pursue the demon who caused this misery, until he or I shall perish in mortal conflict. I call on you, spirits of the dead, to aid me in my work."

You are answered through the stillness of the night by a loud and fiendish laugh. The laughter dies away, and a well-known and abhorred voice, apparently close to your ear, addresses you in an audible whisper. "I am satisfied, miserable wretch! You have determined to take your revenge on me, and the chase shall bring me joy."

You dart toward the spot from which the sound proceeds, but the devil eludes your grasp.

You pursue him. You follow him down the Rhône River to the blue Mediterranean Sea. By a strange chance, you see the fiend enter by night and hide himself in a vessel headed for the Black Sea. You board the same ship, but he escapes.

Through the wilds of Tartary and Russia, you ever follow in his track. The snows descend on your head, and you see the print of his huge step on the white plain.

He leaves marks in writing on the bark of the trees or cut in stone that guide you and fuel your fury. "My reign is not yet over. Follow me; I seek the everlasting ices of the north, where you will feel the misery of cold and frost, to which I am impassive." He even leaves you food so that you may keep pace with his monstrous flight.

You procure a sledge and dogs and thus travel through the snows with inconceivable speed. The biting cold threatens to freeze you before you collect your prize. Soon, you pass from land onto the frozen sea, toward the very top of the Earth—the North Pole! You double your pursuit in this new environment, knowing that your provisions shall soon run out. You close in on him.

Almost within grasp of your foe, your hopes are suddenly extinguished. The wind rises; the sea roars; and, like the mighty shock of an earthquake, it cracks and splits with a tremendous and overwhelming sound. In a few minutes, a tumultuous sea rolls between you and your enemy, and you are left drifting on a scattered piece of ice that is continually lessening and thus preparing for you a hideous death.

In this manner many appalling hours pass; several of your dogs die, and you are about to sink under the accumulation of distress.

You see a ship—and the hope of life. You quickly destroy part of your sledge to construct oars, and exhaustingly move your ice raft in the direction of the ship. You hope to convince the ship's captain to grant you a boat with which you can pursue your enemy. But you are weak and cannot fight the shipmen when they pull you aboard.

Your pursuit is now at an end—unfulfilled. You feel the life drain from you. You see the captain's thirst for scientific knowledge is as great as yours. As a warning, you tell the captain your story, so that he may not make the same mistakes as a man of science that you have. You spend your last breath convincing him to swear to destroy your creation if ever he should encounter him.

And then you die.

Your creation sneaks upon the ship and is filled with

remorse and regret after seeing your dead body—the body of his creator. His journey, too, is at an end.

Promising the captain that humanity will never see him again, he springs from the cabin window onto an ice raft, which lies close to the vessel. He is soon taken away by the waves and lost in darkness and distance.

THE END

ou are delighted to know that your dearest friend waits for you behind your closed door. You have faith that both your friend and your creation can meet each other without ill consequence.

"Henry, please do come in!" you say, acting overly jovial for the sake of making your creation feel happy. "We were just having breakfast!"

Henry enters with an equally jovial laugh and then asks, "We? Who is with you this morning, good Doctor?"

You embrace Henry fully, overwhelmed with emotions, holding him perhaps a little longer than necessary so that he may not yet regard your creation. "Clerval, it delights me to see you. And, please, I am not yet a doctor. Though I will soon be considered one of the greatest, as is evident from who sits at my table."

Your embrace comes to an end, and Clerval gasps upon finally observing the creature.

"Frankenstein, who—" he stammers, "—what? What is that . . . thing?"

He regards Henry with his yellow eyes and begins to growl and shake in his chair.

You swiftly reassure your creation. "This is my friend. FRIEND." You emphasize the word.

"Embrace me once again, Clerval," I say. "Quickly now, we must prove you are 'friend' visually. He has not yet learned much vocabulary. I created him last night, you see . . ."

"Of course," says Henry, still shocked. He embraces you.

The creature seems satisfied, and he continues to devour his fifth plate of eggs.

"You will sit with us then, friend?" you ask Henry. "Please do join us for breakfast. I must hear about your journey, and how you convinced your father that coming here would be a benefit to you."

You sit at the breakfast table in silence for some time. Henry looks at the creature. He is getting better at eating his eggs (without breaking the plate), and you sit smiling at Clerval.

"Oh, I nearly forgot," Clerval says as he hands you a note. "A captain . . . von Hindenburg, I believe . . . of the Prussian Army was outside your apartment. He handed me this note. He said something about wanting to use your skills to create an army. Do you think he means for you to join the army?"

You couldn't care less, though you snatch up the note

and bury it in your papers for future reference. "Is he not a thing of beauty?" you ask.

Clerval responds with another question. "Frankenstein, did you say you *made* him?"

"Indeed!" you reply. "I pieced him together from various fresh corpses I found in Ingolstadt's graveyards. It was one of the hardest labors I have ever undertaken in my life. And finally, last night . . . he came to life! You will have to pardon his appearance. I must admit that, it being my first attempt, I was not sure of how many materials I would need . . ."

"Materials?" asked Clerval.

"Yes, materials," you reply. "Body parts. Muscles. Organs. Tissues. Skin shrinks so terribly, I had to build a new machine that stretches it just to get enough on him. And next time, I must be better about how I stitch him together. Those damnable stitches are what make him look the most . . . what is the word?"

"Gruesome," replies Clerval.

The creature lets out a guttural cry and lifts his hand up to his face. Where his index finger should be is a bloody stump.

"No!" you say. "He has cut his finger off. Where is it?"

Clerval points to the plate. Among the eggs and bacon is a bloody index finger. You collect it and say, "I must rush into my laboratory and grab the instruments required to fix his . . . accident. Would you mind watching him for a brief minute?"

"Frankenstein, I know not—"

Before Clerval can finish, you leave the room, and return to find all is well. You rush to your creation and begin to stitch up the finger. He picks at the last of the bacon with his good hand.

"Frankenstein," says Clerval slowly so as not to disturb your concentration, "this creature you have created is so raw. Certainly the people at the university could help you perfect it? It seems as though he will need much work before he is ready to be part of society; not just his physical demeanor but his mental as well."

"You speak the truth, Clerval," you say. "He will need much work. Last night, as I slept fitfully with this creature on my lap, I was convinced that the first step would be to seek the advice of colleagues at the university. However, I see now that we must be cautious. His perturbed reaction to your knock on my door brought me to this conclusion. I let you inside today because I knew that you among all the souls on earth could keep my secret. And I now believe that until we have perfected my creation, we must not let anyone know of him or of the work that led to him."

"But I am no scientist!" Henry laments. "Frankenstein, what would you have me do? Will I need to pursue that course of study at this university?"

"No, no, you misunderstand me," you say. You finish sewing the creature's finger and put all of your focus on Clerval.

"I need not a scientist at this hour," you continue. "I need a gentleman; and I can think of no greater gentleman than you. By your example, this creature will realize what it means to be a gentleman, and that is why I need you to help me. My experiment will not succeed until I have matched a sound mind with his sound body. I shall focus on his body, and you on his mind."

"Very well," says Clerval, "I will help you in this endeavor, though I shall not let my studies decline! I came to the university to learn, and learn I shall, but I shall also help you. I promise, your secret is well-kept with me."

"Excellent," you say, happy that you have a friend and confidant to help you with your labors. "Then let us begin! Show him how to eat like a gentleman."

After doling out another generous portion of eggs for each of your guests, you draw the creature's attention to Clerval. He puts a napkin on his lap, daintily picks up a fork, and begins to eat his eggs as a gentleman would. The creature witnesses how Clerval behaves and tries his best to do the same. By the end of the breakfast, your creature's egg-eating has greatly improved.

This is the first of many lessons that you and Clerval give your creation. Clerval moves into your apartment, and you transform your laboratory into a bedchamber for Clerval and the creature, so that he can watch, and mimic, Clerval throughout the day. You arrange your schedules so that one of you is always at the apartment with him.

Turn to page 41

"**N**othing you say can convince me not to destroy what I have created!" you say.

You throw yourself at him. He easily holds you at arm's length, laughing a terrible laugh. You growl at him in return. The echo of your outbursts causes snow to crash down the mountain.

His strength is so great that for a moment you nearly relent, amazed as you are by the abilities that you brought to life.

"You think you can destroy me? Ha!" his laughing increases.

"If you shall not allow me to destroy you, then destroy me," you growl.

"Man, you shall live!" he says. "So that you may give me what I wish."

Though he has you by the neck, your arms are free. You swiftly reach into your back pocket for a blade, grasp it firmly, and swing it into his chest.

He roars and throws you off him. You tumble back into a crevasse, the echoes of his anger following you all the way to the bottom, and your death.

THE END

You determine to embrace your creation.

You live off the meat it hunts and brings to you at the hut you have erected for yourself at the base of Mont Blanc. It is playful as a puppy, and as you grow older, its strength does not wane.

You lose sight of all society and your time bound up in it. You become a hermit, avoiding anyone who may come close to you. Though you know you have made the right decision, still you live in constant angst that the hound may grow tired of you and devour you. At times it regards you with its dead eyes in a way that makes you shiver.

However, you catch a fever and die swiftly before it ever changes its mind about you.

Hikers attempting to summit Mont Blanc speak of a mysterious howl they hear when the wind is high. It is your creation mourning the loss of its master.

THE END

You will ask for help from Elizabeth. You are energized with the thought of seeing her. Yes! You may be a broken man, but Elizabeth shall save you, you are sure of it!

Even if she stopped to rest, she could make it to you in three days by carriage. A letter would reach her in roughly the same time. So you have a mere five days to come up with a plan and determine how to get a letter to her.

But where am I? you think.

You wander the camp and listen to the conversations of soldiers, careful that von Hindenburg is not nearby to witness your lack of labor. After some time, you determine that you are not far from Verdun on the Meuse River.

You write a letter filled with passion, praising her beauty and gentleness, presenting her with your predicament, and calling upon her to come to your aid without delay. Once in Verdun, she must convince the local parish to ring the church bells for three minutes. Knowing she is there, you will make your escape and meet her on the bridge over the Meuse River.

Now you must send the letter out without it being seen. Von Hindenburg would most certainly destroy any missive written in your hand.

Surely the soldiers must be able to send post to their families, you think. You make your way back to the tents of those soldiers who you heard before speak in soft tones of faraway loves. Your search bears no fruit—you see no one writing letters.

You panic. If you don't send your letter today, you must present von Hindenburg with his one hundred soldiers or face death—and you have not even picked up a tool in five days! Your choice, however, is made, and there is no going back. You double your efforts to find out how post gets sent from this damnable place and, in a stroke of luck, you find a soldier carrying a packet of letters. You walk into him on purpose.

"Watch where you walk!" he growls, and the letters fly. You toss your letter in the flutter of falling post and drop to the ground to gather the fallen letters with haste.

"I do beg your forgiveness," you say, trying hard not to smile. "So deep in thought was I that I neglected to see you there."

"You very well saw me," replies the soldier. He swears loudly. Other soldiers begin to look. Your joy at having such a stroke of luck soon melts into worry. You do not wish to draw attention to yourself.

"What is this?!" booms a voice. You turn on your hands and knees to see shiny boots before you. You look up.

"Von Hindenburg!" you yelp.

"You will address me as Herr Kapitän, Frankenstein." The captain's towering figure looms over you as you grab the last letter—your letter—and put it at the bottom of the pile.

Von Hindenburg pulls you off the ground by lifting your chin with his riding crop. You hand the soldier the letters, and he is dismissed.

"Why are you not in your laboratory?" growls von Hindenburg. "You have much work to do, do you not, Herr Doktor?"

"Yes, Herr Kapitän," you say, wishing to remove yourself from the situation as quickly as possible. "Just a momentary break. I have fifty men for you already . . ."

And off you flee, back to the laboratory. You dare not even look back.

You lock yourself in your laboratory and feverishly await Elizabeth's signal. Five days pass. You are exhausted from lack of sleep. You are terrified von Hindenburg will inspect your work early. There is nothing to show! Elizabeth's coming is assured, but what if she runs into something upon the road? Another strike of lightning felling another tree?

Then you hear them . . . the bells!

You count the minutes . . . one . . . two . . . three! It is she! The sun sets and the guards of the camp are changing. You have had nothing but time to plot your escape, piecing together the steps that you should take in order to slip away unnoticed, and now is the time to give your plan life.

You swiftly leave the camp and mount the hill ahead. On the other side, you see the river. You look back to see no one following, and sprint down the hill. On the bridge ahead, a carriage! And the beauteous figure of your love, Elizabeth.

You wave joyously, and she is lifting her hand with a smile to do the same when she is suddenly struck with a look of terror.

"Cousin!" she shrieks. "Behind you!"

You turn to see von Hindenburg descending the hill with his rifle. He stops and raises it. A shot rings out . . .

. . . and von Hindenburg clutches his leg and falls. Soldiers appear at the top of the hill and surround their fallen captain. However, instead of assisting him, they shackle him.

You look back to the bridge, and standing next to Elizabeth, his rifle raised, is your dear brother Ernest!

He lowers it and you run to the bridge.

"Ernest!" you cry. "You have saved me."

"You are mistaken, brother." Ernest points to Elizabeth. "It is she who has saved you."

After a rejuvenating embrace, Elizabeth tells you all.

"When you wrote of your predicament," she said, "I immediately went to your father. He reported the evil that von Hindenburg was attempting to release on the battlefield to the Prussian consulate in Geneva, and they blessed our rescue. I am so very glad I brought Ernest with me, for though the Prussians gave us safe and swift passage, they swore they would not shoot one of their own. Though he will go to trial. And your trial is over!"

You are overjoyed.

You make your way back to Geneva, where you follow in your father's footsteps to become a great statesman. You and Elizabeth have many children and live a comfortable life on the shores of Lake Geneva. Your children are the only new life you ever create.

THE END

ou regard the eyes of the beast and speak soothingly.

"Good dog," you say. "I beg forgiveness that I have no proper food for you. Give me but a little time, and I shall feed you well!"

As you speak, you slowly back away, until you reach the equipment table at the back of the room. You hit the table with a clatter, and the beast growls angrily.

"Worry not," you say, as if to a frightened puppy during a thunderstorm.

You reach behind you and grasp a sharp cutting instrument from the table. But just as you are about to swing it in front of you, the hound pounces with a great growl.

With a scream, you are knocked to the ground. You grip the blade tightly and slash the throat of the beast. There is a clang of metal. You merely graze the knife across the sutures where you connected the head to the body.

The beast clamps down on your arm with a terrible

crunch. The pain is excruciating, and you scream. The hound secures its grasp and whips you around as a young child would a rag doll.

It lets you go, and you roll across the floor in pain, defenseless, weeping. The beast looks you in the eye but once more before it leans down, opens its cavernous mouth, places your head inside, and crushes it like a vise. The last thought in your broken head is one of pride. *Stronger than I could have ever imagined*, you think.

You die.

THE END

You say not a word, for you cannot imagine what would happen if you brought your dear old friend and your creation together.

In fact, this action solidifies in your mind that you must not speak to anyone at all. You ignore callers. You ignore all the letters that you receive from Elizabeth and your father. You know only your work, and it is hard work.

Barring a few trips into town for sundries and vittles, you spend months on end with your creation, though you cannot seem to do more than improve upon his physical appearance. His mental state is not improving. You practice reanimating some frogs to see if you can gain any insight, but none emerge.

Over time, your creation realizes that there is an outside world. Late one night after you have collapsed from exhaustion, he heads off into town. You are awoken by screaming. The citizens of Ingolstadt, frightened by his size and likeness, descend upon him. This angry mob tears him to pieces with pitchforks and burns him with torches.

You can do nothing, for hastening to assist him will reveal that you are indeed his creator.

For days, you mourn the loss of your creation. You are too proud to return to your family, but you cannot go on like this alone. You wallow in despair for sad days and sleepless nights, until finally, you get a burst of inspiration.

I could create a large hound! you think. *Yes, something that is strong but naturally obedient. I could train it—and in it find companionship!*

You scour the alleyways and yards of Ingolstadt, but have a hard time finding large enough "specimens" for your "experiment."

Turn to page 108

*T*hough it rankles you so, you would rather see your creation reach his full potential than rip him from the solace and knowledge that has been given him by Elizabeth.

Things proceed normally for a number of weeks. You are once again lost in your studies.

Each modification you make on Leon drives you to create something new—some way to better him.

With Elizabeth busy with Leon, your life is nothing but work. In fact, you are completely distracted when Elizabeth enters your laboratory one day.

"Dear Frankenstein," she says. "I must speak with you."

"Can it wait?" you say, closely examining a new piece of tissue on your slab.

"Darling, please," says Elizabeth. "I promise you, after I speak with you, I shan't have need to bother you again."

"What?" Suddenly all of your senses are on Elizabeth. "What is this, Elizabeth?"

Your stomach fills with fire, for you know even before she tells you.

"I am in love with Leon," she says.

A great silence fills the room. It is broken by a knock at the door.

"Have you told him?" asks Leon from behind the door. "I cannot bear to see him. Let him know that it wounds our very souls to harm him in this way, but that we are indeed in love."

You are enraged. "How can *you* love?" you bellow at the door. "You are incapable. Monster! Be gone!"

"But, Father," Leon says. He enters the room on his knees. "It is you who taught me how to love and, chiefly, how to love Elizabeth. Even before I learned to speak, oh, how you spoke about her! So all I have ever known is to love Elizabeth. When she came and told me that in fact she felt the same way, why . . . I could move mountains for her."

"Love is strange," says Elizabeth. "I can scarcely describe to you my feelings for Leon and why I love him. It is easier for you to explain to me how to create life from death—yours is a science that is possible to explain. Mine is an emotion that overtakes me without reason. Cousin, you should take great pride in the fact that you created something that would produce such a great love in me!"

"Father," continues Leon, "I am deeply grateful to you for creating me! I know that your work is like standing on the edge of a cliff. I cannot, knowing all I now know, believe that you were able to step up to the precipice of knowledge to see what was possible without going too far, or slipping, and dashing yourself on the rocks below in the effort. I will always be grateful for your genius."

"How dare you!?" you say. "I am your father—nay, your creator, your god! I gave you life, I gave you knowledge to make the most of that life, skills and manners, the proper clothes. I even allowed Elizabeth to tutor you despite the risk. And how do you repay me? In kind? Nay, you steal my love from me."

You leave the room in a fury. You retreat to your bedroom, sullen and forlorn. You lie for hours on end, thinking only of your lost love, and of the traitor. Elizabeth knocks on your door.

"Leave me be!" you yell.

The monster pleads with you through the door. You moan loudly to drown out his entreaties.

For days this continues until you are mad with jealousy! You must do something! But what?

If you abandon your creation and Elizabeth, turn to page 119

If you make a new "Elizabeth," turn to page 113

In a dreary night of late November, you behold the accomplishment of your toils. With an anxiety that almost amounts to agony, you collect the instruments of life around you, that you might use to infuse a spark of being into the lifeless matter that lays at your feet. You sew together the body parts you have stolen from the grave and charge your galvanizing tools.

At first, your tools fail you. But, determined to master your craft, you continue. It is already one in the morning; the rain patters dismally against the panes, and your candle is nearly burnt out, when, by the glimmer of the half-extinguished light, you see the dull, yellow eye of the creature open; it breathes hard, and a convulsive motion agitates its limbs.

"It is alive!" you exclaim in triumph. "It . . . is . . . ALLLIIIIIVE!"

You have achieved the very goal with which you set out.

You look your creation in the eye, but just as suddenly and surely as he awakes to new life, a new thought is born in your head. You cannot describe the feeling that takes over the jolt of triumph that just coursed through your frame. You have taken infinite pains and care to form new life, but have created a wretch! His limbs are in proportion, and you selected his features as beautiful. Beautiful! Great God! His yellow skin scarcely covers his muscles and arteries beneath; his hair is of a lustrous black, and flowing; his teeth of pearly whiteness; but this only forms a more horrid contrast with his dull, watery eyes, his shriveled complexion, and straight black lips.

You have worked hard to infuse life into an inanimate body. For this, you have deprived yourself of rest and health. But now that you have finished, your dream vanishes, and breathless horror and disgust fill your heart. Unable to deal with the being you have created, you rush out of the room and throw yourself onto the bed in your clothes, endeavoring to seek a few moments of forgetfulness.

You wake from your sleep with horror; cold sweat covers your forehead, your teeth chatter, and every limb shakes; when, by the dim yellow light of the moon, you see the wretch—the miserable monster whom you have created. His eyes, yellow and dead in appearance, are fixed on you. His jaw opens, and he mutters some sounds, while a grin wrinkles his cheeks. One hand is stretched out toward you.

You, Victor Frankenstein, are at a complete loss. You are frozen in fear. You are overwhelmed by exhaustion. You are not sure if your creature reaches for you because he intends you harm or because he needs your help!

Your mind seethes with a million questions. What is your creature's nature? Good, despite his appearance? Could he be made even better with your tutelage?

Or is the mind of this wretch you have created just as scarred and terrible as his body? Should you run to save yourself from your damned creation?

If you run from your creation,
turn to page 105

**If you try to speak with your creation
and learn how you can help him,**
turn to page 30

Elizabeth is right. Your cruelty, and the cruelty of those whom the wretch encountered on his journey, made him a monster.

As you knew he would, the creature appears at the window to witness her birth. Elizabeth brings her gently to life.

She rises slowly from the slab. She seems confused, but Elizabeth is there to soothe her. Your first creation, upset at any delay in being joined with his new bride, rushes through the front door and attempts to embrace her.

The bride moans. You worry that Elizabeth shall be harmed by the monster, for he only has eyes for his new bride, and Elizabeth is in the way.

But Elizabeth calms him by saying, "You must be gentle with her, as my husband, Victor, should have been with you when you were first born. Give her time. She moans not because of your face but because she is confused. Take her not from us, but rather let us help you both."

Elizabeth proves to be an adept scientist and counselor.

"She may have been created for you," she counsels your original creation, "but she is her own creature. Forget not as you seek out peace and joy from her that you would do well to bring her joy and peace as well. Be kind to each other."

She assures that the new companions are able to enjoy their lives. They disappear into the wilds, never to be seen again.

You and Elizabeth live long and wonderful lives, both becoming scientists of note and using what you have learned for the betterment of all mankind.

You die before Elizabeth. At your funeral, not only do Elizabeth, numerous children, and grandchildren mourn you, but far in the back of the church, two tall cloaked figures weep at your loss.

You are remembered as a great man. Elizabeth is remembered as a greater woman.

THE END

"**V**ery well, then," you say swiftly. "It shall be done!"

You make your way home as quickly as possible, with only one burning thought on your mind—escape for you and your sweet Elizabeth!

Upon your return to your father's home, without a word to your family, you rush to Elizabeth and plead with her.

"Elizabeth, I know that a woman of your morals would rather a wedding in the style and grace to which you are accustomed. However, I must impress upon you that we are both in great danger and must leave Geneva tonight."

"Oh, dear Victor, what is it?" she cries. "When you left, I thought that your wanderings would make you calmer and better, and yet this dark, funereal rage seems to have deepened into anxiety and paranoia. Let me speak at once with your father."

You hold her tightly in your arms. "No, Elizabeth, the

time is now. You must come with me. We must flee this place. For all I know, my father and Ernest are already dead. For *he* is watching."

"Good God, Victor, you are mad! I must get a doctor at once."

She rushes out of the room. You follow in pursuit, but are immediately stopped by your creation.

"Frankenstein!" he bellows. "You have deceived me! You mean to flee? Do you truly believe you can escape me? You should know, having made me, how much more powerful I am than you. Now that you have shown your true intent, I have no other choice than to turn against the vile humanity of which you are a part."

You realize you have made the wrong decision. You throw yourself upon him.

"Kill me and be satisfied," you beg him, "Leave humanity alone—I alone should be punished!"

He merely picks you up, tosses you upon the ground, and says, "Man, I *shall* punish you! I shall let you live on, so that you may witness all my victims perishing before you and be tortured by it."

He runs away. You crumple into a heap. When Elizabeth comes back, she brings with her a physician, who immediately counsels her to have you put into an insane asylum.

At first, you are visited by your family and friends, but one day they no longer come.

And though you incessantly wail that it is your creation that has destroyed them, your attendants do nothing but stare at you—and tighten your straitjacket.

You spend your remaining days cursing the hour of your birth, spiraling deeper into madness, until finally losing your mind completely.

You wither away and die.

THE END

No. You shall have none of this. Elizabeth is yours. Not this . . . "Leon's." You vow never to call him by that name and storm into the room.

"Excuse me, Elizabeth," you say. "I need to work with him. Right now."

"But, cousin, I must finish his daily less—"

"Now, Elizabeth!"

You bring him to your laboratory, sit him on the slab, and tell him, "You have learned enough. It is time for you to go. I can no longer have you near Elizabeth."

Your monster looks sad. For a moment, you are proud that his emotions are working so well. But you press on unperturbed.

"No," you say, shaking your head. "I insist! I know you have formed a bond with her, but she is mine."

He flees your apartment, and you return to Elizabeth. "But, my dear cousin, where is he?" she asks.

"I am sorry to say, my dear, that he has decided to leave us."

She begins to weep. You embrace her and are filled with joy that she has returned once again to your arms.

Two weeks later, there comes a loud knock at your door. Elizabeth and Henry are out in the countryside. You, meanwhile, are continuing your studies, trying hard to remember—with your subject gone—what you did to create life. You open the door. The monster enters, and he is filled with rage.

"You have shunned me," says he. "And I can abide only if you allow me one request. You must make a companion for me. If I cannot have Elizabeth, then you must provide me with someone who can take her place. I demand a bride to live with in peace, away from the prying eyes of humanity—for I wish not to see the likes of you again! If you refuse, then I will bring down upon you a reign of terror until the end of your days and will destroy all you hold dear. I will become a plague on humanity."

You relent and determine that your best course of action is to bend to his demands. Loathsome though it is, you feel you owe him this one prize.

You, along with Clerval, journey to England so that you may hear from scientists at Oxford the latest techniques that may assist you. You travel to visit friends in Scotland, staying in Edinburgh and then Perth. It is there that you tell Clerval you wish to continue your journey alone. You retreat to a hut on a nearly desolate Scottish island to begin your labors unseen, though you do not doubt the monster follows you to assure your work indeed progresses. You soon find another grotesque creation before you—ready to be brought to life! As you have suspected he would, your monster appears at the window to witness the birth of his bride.

Turn to page 23

"**D**ear Henry," you say, "I am so grateful for everything you have done for me, but you are correct. I have asked too much of you. Yes, it should be me that is the sole bearer of this weight."

Clerval is greatly relieved that you are willing to take on his duties. He continues on with his studies while you do your best to bring your creature's mental capacity to its fullest potential.

Clerval has already done much great work, and it would have continued on apace were it not so frustrating. You soon find that you, too, are not suited to the work required. You are able to create a companion of sorts in your monster—someone with whom you can share a laugh or a smile. But your hard work never brings him to the point where you are able to introduce him to anyone else.

In fact, you spend so much time trying to better him physically and mentally that you begin to ignore not only

Clerval but your family in Geneva. Letters from Elizabeth remain sealed, and soon she believes you have spurned her for another. This, in a sense, is true, as you are so obsessed with bettering your monster, and yet so incapable of doing so, that he truly is the only thing you have time for in your life.

You move to a small village outside of Ingolstadt and, in the darkness of a moonless night, bring the monster there so that you may have more space to take care of him. It is exhausting work. Still, you never seek assistance—both to protect your secret and because of your great pride.

Time goes by swiftly. You grow old, but the monster maintains the strength with which you imbued him. Upon your deathbed, you are proud that your monster cares for you so tenderly—just as you had spent your entire life caring for him. Your dying words both soothe the monster and give him a plan for how to live his life away from the prying eyes of others. Even with what little skill you know he has, he will be able to keep himself safe.

You die feeling that you have done great work—even though none shall ever know of it.

THE END

You live out a meager existence in the rural German countryside, slowly traveling from town to town northward and away from Geneva. The monster never finds you, and you hope he never finds your family.

In just a few years, you die alone from the plentiful diseases of the patients to whom you tend as the itinerant doctor.

THE END

nother knock at the door further distracts the dog. Though your feverish mind is paralyzed with fear, you will your body to react. You flee past the dog, toward your laboratory and the tools that may indeed save you. The demon follows in quick pursuit. It knocks you down with its enormous paws at the entrance of your laboratory.

The dog grabs you by your neck, piercing your skin, making blood flow.

"Noooooooo," you say, but the beast swings its head around, and you with it. You hear your neck bones crack.

It drags you back into the parlor and spits you out onto the floor. Your face hits the hardwood.

As you roll over, the demon dog lifts its cadaverous head high and howls. With a flash of drooly teeth, it brings its muzzle down upon your stomach and bites hard. It feels as if your whole body is trapped in its jaws. You beat your hands upon its head, but in vain. With each pound on its massively large skull, you lose energy.

Soon, in shock and dying, your horror changes to admiration. *Well, I did indeed make him strong,* you think. *It is a pity I shall never be able to share what I have learned and change science forever.*

The last sound you hear before you die is the crunch of your bones in the demon dog's mouth.

THE END

You journey south to your homeland with the swiftest horses you can purchase. As you get closer, you do indeed see signs of the hound—great deer massacred on the road, their flesh torn by terrible teeth. You are so sure that it has arrived in Geneva before you that you are happily shocked to be jovially welcomed by your family when you arrive.

You wish nothing more than to relate that your family's ruin is near, but you remain calm.

Your younger brother, William, bounds upon you and shrieks with joy. Elizabeth, looking as beautiful as ever, embraces you. Your older brother, Ernest, and your father are surprised by your sudden entry into the home. You cannot tell them why you are there, but you tell them that you saw a terribly monstrous hound just before you arrived.

You counsel them to stay inside. Your family scoffs at the idea.

"My dear son," says your father, "enough of this hound. What of Henry Clerval? Why did he not journey home with you?"

You feel deep guilt pour forth from your very heart. As pained as you are by his passing, you must never reveal the truth of what happened to Clerval, lest you be seen as mad.

"Henry?" you lie. "Why, I never saw him in Ingolstadt!"

You cannot mourn Clerval, as your mind is focused on nothing but your demon dog. You are in a constant state of concealed panic. You manage to keep your entire family in the house for the length of a week, but run out of excuses for why you wish them to keep doing so. Though the hound has not made itself known, you know you must not ignore it. You have not yet sought it out, worried about what shall happen if you leave your family home without you.

You determine that your immediate union with dear Elizabeth would be the best course of action: You may remain constantly by her side. You propose to Elizabeth, and she is overjoyed. You convince your father, frail in his old age, to transfer William into the care of you and Elizabeth.

You marry swiftly and, after a celebration, begin a long honeymoon journey around Lake Geneva. What joy Elizabeth brings you! Life is so full of bliss that you forget you ever created a hound.

But your creation forgets you not. It appears one evening like an apparition, so surprising in its appearance that it destroys Elizabeth before you may even take up arms against it.

Filled with sadness and shame, you leave the body of your wife and hunt the beast, cursing yourself that you did not sooner. It toys with you by scaling Alpine peaks you cannot reach, but stays close enough that you can pursue it. You know not if you can continue.

You press on for weeks. You are so engaged in the capture of your creation that you do not attend Elizabeth's funeral, failing to console your loved ones for the loss of someone so dear to all. Your father, furious that you could not defend Elizabeth and then fled what he sees as your responsibility, sends you a letter telling you he has forever banished you from his home. You do not argue—it is a fitting punishment.

But your determination pays off. Though the hound taunts you, allowing you to get close, but never close enough, you study its mannerisms intently. You determine how to capture it near the summit of Mont Blanc, where it has slowly been leading you for the past weeks.

You approach it fully prepared to fight. Your body trembles, nay, aches for the action! Now the moment is finally at hand. You rush at it, with a galvanizing tool capable of immediate death, but it snatches it out of your hand before you can complete your task. It flings it, runs after it, and with a great crunch, removes all power from it. It stares at you from a distance.

"Demon dog," you shriek, your voice reverberating off the summit of Mont Blanc. "You have bested me. I shall die proud that I created something so strong and cunning. Finish me now, then!"

The dog cocks its head as if trying to understand what you say. It runs at you, and you close your eyes, ready for its fatal blow.

But nothing happens. You open your eyes. The dog, wagging its tail, has placed the tool back at your feet. It regards you with anticipation. It wishes to play with you! You pick the tool up and throw it. The hound fetches it and returns it once again. This time it allows you to take it directly from its mouth.

You regard the mangled tool in your hands and are surprised to see that it has regained a small charge. In the dog's state of play, and with this bit of energy, you could dispatch the beast easily.

But why kill it? You have nothing left. Clerval is gone. Elizabeth is gone. Your family has disowned you. The dog's murderous rage was merely a game it played with its master. You dare not think of what might have been avoided if you had merely tossed it a ball many weeks ago.

You are unsure you have the power to kill it . . . Should you just embrace it? As terrible as it is, it is all you are left with in this abhorrent world into which you have plunged.

If you decide to embrace your creation, turn to page 57

If you attempt to destroy your creation, turn to page 123

"I must absolutely insist," you say. "I must work under the conditions and with the time that I need to give you the proper result."

In an instant, von Hindenburg's face turns an unearthly red. "Sergeant!" he calls.

A soldier approaches.

"Find Igor. Take him and Frankenstein to the French under our white banner. Let them know it is they who created the monsters. Assure them it was a mistake on our part. Collect any prisoners you may manage to negotiate in return for them. Let the French know *these two wretches are meaningless to us.*"

"No!" you cry. "No, I—"

"You have made your decision," says von Hindenburg. "And, frankly, this has been such a bother that I know not if it is worth the effort. There are others like you. Perhaps they can be groomed in time. But we are too busy right now with the French Republic. Goodbye, Herr Frankenstein."

"No! Nooooo!" you yell.

You are carried off kicking and screaming. Igor soon joins you. The French, knowing that it is you who are responsible for the carnage of their soldiers, eagerly take you in. They spit and jeer at you as they take the time to weigh which extreme punishment is befitting of your unnatural work.

You make your way to the guillotine.

Your head rolls. Like any good assistant, Igor is soon to follow.

THE END

"I fear losing you above all else!" you exclaim. "I fear it more than death."

"But Victor," she replies in her soft tone. "I am yours now! What harm can come to us now that we are together?"

"If I have it my way, no harm shall ever come to us."

You guide Elizabeth to the bedroom. "I must guard you now. You go to sleep, but I shall stay up and watch over you."

Elizabeth, worried by your behavior, hesitates but agrees with your plan. You kiss her forehead gently, tuck her into bed, and then post watch in the room. At the darkest point of night, your monster fulfills his loathsome promise. He creeps in through the window, but you are ready for him. You raise your pistol and shoot. He roars and tumbles into the room, lashing out at you.

Elizabeth is swiftly awoken from her slumber and screams.

The monster growls, "Do you really think your guns and knives can kill me? You know better than anyone that I am strong, for you have made me that way!"

"Yes, but as your creator, I know your weaknesses better than anyone!"

You beg Elizabeth to flee, but terror roots her to the bed.

You fire shot after shot into the beast, but he will not relent. He flings himself on Elizabeth and attempts to choke the life out of your new bride. You spring upon him and plunge a dagger deep into his back. He shudders, releases his grip, and slides slowly off Elizabeth onto the bed.

"Elizabeth, come to me!" you say, reaching for her. As you pull her off the bed, the monster comes once again to life and pulls her back to him. He puts his mouth over her ear and hisses his last words: "He said it himself. He created me. Flee from him, for he is the evil one, not I!"

He dies. You pull Elizabeth off the bed and attempt to console her, but she pushes you away.

"You created him? What does he mean? What did you do to that man? You created him? As God would a man!? Did you disfigure him so? Did you imbue him with such unearthly strength?"

She touches her bruised throat, and her fear melts into sadness.

"Oh my God," she declares. "This was the method of

William's death. You were convinced of Justine's innocence, for you knew it was your monster!"

"Elizabeth, please, let me explain!" Again you try to embrace her. Again she pushes you away.

"Murderer!" She flees from the room. It is the last you ever see of your beloved Elizabeth.

Knowing she herself would sound a raving lunatic if she told the authorities what she knows, she speaks not a word of what you have done. However, she does tell your father, who banishes you. He dies soon thereafter of grief, having lost two sons. Ernest makes sure you never see the house— or your share of the family's fortune—again.

Even in death, your creation gets his wish of your utter sorrow. You die poor, homeless, and hungry, far from your loved ones.

THE END

ou must finish your gruesome task first. Then you shall be ready to marry Elizabeth and enjoy the peace that union brings.

Driven by the thought of bringing your torture to an end and starting life anew, you formulate a plan. You shall travel to England to be far from your family while undertaking your unholy work and to gain tutelage from noted scientists there—and thus assure your task is successful. Before you set off for England, however, your father and Elizabeth—greatly worried about you—conspire to ensure you have a travel companion. They ask dear Henry Clerval to join you.

You meet him in Strasbourg, and as you travel north along the Rhine and on to England and the glorious city of London, Clerval brings great joy to you. From there, you visit the learned men of Oxford, and then head farther north to the Scottish city of Edinburgh. For some time, you forget the gruesome labor ahead, and merely enjoy Clerval's company.

During your journey through Scotland, you stop in the city of Perth to meet an old friend.

Now is the time you must leave Clerval behind to proceed with your unholy work alone.

You tell Clerval that you wish to make the remainder of your tour of Scotland alone. You say, "I may be absent a month or two; but leave me to peace and when I return, I hope it will be with a lighter heart."

You determine to visit some remote spot of Scotland and finish your work in solitude. You do not doubt that the monster follows you and will visit you when you finish, so he may receive his companion.

You travel through the northern highlands and settle on one of the remotest of the Orkney Islands. It is a place fitted for such work, being hardly more than a rock whose high sides are continually beaten upon by the waves. On the whole island there are but three miserable huts, and one of these is vacant when you arrive. You take possession of it and live unseen and unbothered.

As you proceed in your labor, it becomes every day more horrible to you. It is, indeed, a filthy process in which you are engaged.

As you sit one evening in your laboratory, you consider the effects of what you are now doing. What if the demon has been lying this whole time? What if he never intends to leave Europe? What if the bride disagrees with a plan that was set before she was created? Could she become even more vile and evil than he? What if she refuses to leave Europe? More frightening still, what if they have children?

You tremble and your heart fails within you when, on looking up, you see by the light of the moon the demon at the window. A ghastly grin wrinkles his lips as he gazes upon you, where you sit fulfilling his task. He now comes to claim his companion.

Frozen in fear, you know not what to do . . .

Shall you put an end to this new creation before bringing her to life, and risk the monster's wrath? Or shall you take the monster at his word, bring her to life, and leave him and his new bride to their own devices?

If you destroy his companion,
turn to page 185

If you bring his companion to life,
turn to page 23

ou unclasp Clerval's hand and put it to your heart. Your face turns from joy to despair. You know not where to start.

"But, dear Frankenstein," says he, "what is the matter? It is as if you have seen a spirit. Is something wrong?" His smiling countenance, too, disappears.

"Is something wrong?" you ask bitterly. "Something? Nay, everything is wrong." You twist your hair and sway, overcome by exhaustion at the task of having to reveal your horrific truth.

What if the monster you created is already following you? You must return to your apartment! But what if the monster is there, waiting for you? It matters not. Too many people from the inn are staring at you, and you may pass out from worry and fatigue. You must return to a safe space, to your home, to reveal your terrible secret to Clerval.

In order to ward off the stares of unwanted eyes, you straighten yourself and speak seriously to your companion. "I am so sorry to keep you from unpacking and settling into your new room, friend, but if you could join me immediately at my apartment, I have much I must tell you."

You clasp your hands together, almost as if in prayer, silently begging your friend to join you.

"Yes, of course," Clerval says with a look of uncertainty still upon his pursed lips.

You head swiftly to the university, and your apartment there. You hesitate at the foot of the stairs that lead up to your room.

"Please, Frankenstein, you must tell me what bothers you so," says Clerval.

"In one brief moment, all shall be known," you say. You climb up the stairs, each step feeling harder and harder to complete. By the time you reach the top, Clerval must support you, for you swoon with fear of what lies behind your door.

You must give your friend warning. You stop outside your door.

"Dear, dear Henry," you say, "the fruit of my studies, of my work, may very well lie behind that door. But it is a most rotten fruit."

You enter the apartment and do not find your wicked creation lurking within.

Relieved, you immediately tell your newly arrived confidant everything you have done and what you have unleashed upon the world.

"Good God, Frankenstein!" he says. "What terrors you have been through. But have you indeed created life? That is truly astonishing. You should be so proud!"

"What does it matter," you hiss back, "when that life is so corrupt and filled with evil from its conception?"

"Frankenstein, you know not this creature's true nature! When a baby is born into this world, does it not cry out for months and months before finally coming to its senses and perceiving its surroundings? And does not a man take even longer to realize his purpose on earth? And only then with the help of those older than him?"

You take a moment to think of what Clerval says. Yet, you saw the wretched beast firsthand and know that he has already killed a member of the Prussian Army.

Babies do not murder straight out of the womb, you think to yourself.

You argue about this for some time. Eventually, you both realize that the best thing you can do is head out into the city and find some sign of the wretch in Ingolstadt as soon as possible. You arm yourself with a galvanizing tool small enough that you may carry it. This small but powerful rod of metal, which helped bring life to your creation with a spark of electricity, could also swiftly bring death if you discharge its energies all at once. And that is exactly what you hope to do. You charge it fully in your laboratory, using a hand-cranked electricity generator.

You head out into the streets of the city. You are grateful to have your friend accompany you at such a time, but you do not tell Clerval your true intention, for you do not trust that he, like you, wishes to see the creature die as swiftly as he came to life.

Clerval is a most excellent hunter, and he uses the same skill he possesses to track game in the wild to find little signs as to your creation's whereabouts. You ask people passing by if they have noticed a strange large man. By evening, your endeavors lead to a quiet part of town. You can almost feel him nearby, and your senses sharpen as you lose the light of day.

As you get closer to finding him, your heart swells with the prospect of bringing things swiftly to an end. You find a number of half-eaten chicken carcasses, with their feathers still intact. You point at them and say, "You see, Henry, his is a bloody nature!"

Clerval responds, "But Frankenstein, your creation is just hungry!"

Clues lead you to the very edge of town. An old wall encircles it, and tight, dark alleyways lead to it and to no escape. If only you could trap your monster in one of those corners, then your tool would do the rest of the work.

You raise your galvanizing tool in the air. It crackles ominously. Clerval pushes it down.

"Frankenstein," says Clerval, "what if this creature's nature is indeed one of goodness? Why do we not plan to subdue him rather than destroy him?"

"Henry," you say, "though I appreciate that you see the world in such positive ways, you know not what I saw."

"Dear Victor, I might say that *you* know not what you saw, your mind being so feverish from the work you had completed. Do you not question the fact that you went from elated to horrified in but an instant? It sounds to me that your mind is uneven."

The moon rises, as does the tension between you and Clerval. Before you can continue arguing with your friend, you see ahead in the moon's soft glow the figure of your creation crouched low.

"There he is!" you exclaim. You rush forward.

"Wait, Frankenstein," Clerval says. "Hear my counsel but for a moment more!"

But you do not hear your dear friend's counsel. You corner the frightened but powerful creature, and are just about to strike him when Clerval steps between you and the monster you have created.

"No, Frankenstein!" he pleads. "Let your creation live! Your work is unfinished here! You owe it to humanity to bring him to his fullest potential."

If you listen to Clerval,
turn to page 118

If you insist upon killing your creation,
turn to page 36

You escape and rush downstairs. You take refuge in the courtyard. You walk up and down in the greatest agitation, listening attentively for the approach of the demonical corpse to which you have so miserably given life. A mummy could not be so hideous as that wretch.

You collapse on a bench in the courtyard and sleep fitfully, unsure of where your nightmares end and reality begins. You dream of a terrible rumbling and are awoken by the sound of the courtyard gate opening. You see the monster you created enter from the streets, water running down his face from the cold rain. You shriek in terror.

"Are you real?" you shout. You pull up a cobblestone from the ground and raise it high. "Or but a vision of my madness!?"

But your creation is nowhere to be found. There are several figures at the door, in uniform. They part to allow an imposing military officer into the courtyard.

He turns to the others. "That shall be all," he says. The men salute. The largest of them swings the gate to the courtyard shut.

"I am indeed real," the figure says. "I am Kapitän von Hindenburg of the Prussian Army, and I do very much apologize for disturbing your slumber. We know your work has not left much time for sleep."

The captain takes off his hat, wet from the rain, and stretches out his hand as if to shake yours. You lower the cobblestone.

"Yes," you mumble. "You are real. I suppose you have learned of my wicked deeds and are come to take me away."

"No," he says, and a slight smile curls upon his lips. "I am here to help you with your work. I have a very simple proposal. We have captured the . . . man you created. We are happy to take him off your hands."

"Take him off my hands?" you ask, still groggy, still unsure your vision is real. "You mean . . ."

"Destroy him," says von Hindenburg. "We have been watching you and know of what you are capable. You can do better than that poor soul. And you shall. With us. We have the equipment and"—von Hindenburg chuckles—"materials beyond your wildest dreams. And we are in need of strong men."

"Strong men?" you say. "But I am so weak."

"Yes," says von Hindenburg, a sparkle in his eye. "But you

can *create* such strength. Your man struggled greatly when we came upon him. He killed one of my men and injured three before we were able to subdue him. Your creation is rudimentary, yes. But strong. You have just begun your work, Frankenstein. Join us on the battlefield and create for me the greatest army ever known on earth!"

What this military man proposes is lunacy. Unthinkable. But there would be certain advantages. You would have endless resources. You would be protected by a strong army—one that you could make even stronger. Though you hesitate. "What if I refuse?" you ask.

"We shall release your creation," says von Hindenburg. "And he shall be free to do as he wishes. I assure you, this shall be your last chance to destroy him. Though it shall not be *his* last chance to destroy *you*."

If you agree to von Hindenburg's request, turn to page 127

If you decide to take your chances with your creation set free, turn to page 16

You wrack your brain trying to figure out how you shall find more dog parts. You remember your friend Henry Clerval. As a youth, he once went on a hunt that had dogs to help track prey. Perhaps there is a similar hunting culture in Ingolstadt. You query fellow university students, who reply in the positive.

"Where are those dogs housed when not hunting?" you ask.

Through their answers, you find a kennel, and go there to kidnap a few of the strongest dogs available. You bring them back to your laboratory in the dead of night, careful to avoid the watchful eyes of the local authorities.

You know that what you have done is terrible and gruesome. But you know as well that science will benefit from your labors!

You spend countless nights locked in your laboratory, combining the parts of the dogs you captured into a glorious whole hound. You wield your instruments of life until, finally, one night, you are rewarded with the wag of a tail.

"It is alive!" you scream into the night. "It is ALIVE!"

In response, your creation growls. The teeth that you so masterfully placed in the mouth gleam in the candlelight. The beast rises tentatively off of the table onto all four appendages. Shakily at first, until, with a rippling of muscle, the beast stands steady, and looks deep into your eyes.

"Good boy," you say, though your voice is trembling. You are tired, and this new life appeared so swiftly that you are not ready for it. You have no cage or leash. Discarded dog parts and unused equipment litter your parlor, a hindrance to your swift escape. You curse yourself for the oversight, but thinking quickly, you realize you have other tools to calm the dog. You inch backward to the tank filled with the fruits of your previous labor—your beloved frogs.

"Here, boy," you say, and grab a squirming, growling frog. "You must be hungry!" You toss the fresh meat ahead, and your creation catches it masterfully and gobbles it down in one bite.

It licks its lips, but it regards not the rest of the frogs in the tank. It regards you.

I had not calculated how ravenous it would be! you think, but you must not panic. You look at the sharp instruments on the table and realize that it would probably be easier to kill the beast than to try to feed it. *Yes!* you think. You shall kill it now, and reanimate it once you've dressed the wounds, giving yourself time to plan!

Oh, but why go through the trouble? You have spent countless hours on this creation, lost innumerable hours of sleep. Perhaps if you feed it enough, it could be calmed and dealt with.

If you decide the time has come to kill the beast, turn to page 63

If you decide to continue with the feast of frogs, turn to page 140

"I have no time for this," you growl at the wretched traveler. "My studies are of the utmost importance, especially now that I have such fresh materials at hand. Jean, continue on!"

"But, sir!" croaks the traveler. "How shall I survive the night?"

As your horse's hooves pick up rhythm, you yell back, "Your cloak already provides sufficient warmth. I am sure more travelers shall come down this path—travelers who have not so great a need for swiftness as I!"

You apply constant pressure on Jean and, despite only having one horse, make it to the university early. You meet at once with your advisers to plot out the most beneficial course of study. After a few weeks of research, during which the materials you gathered from the fallen horse are spent, you study the science of anatomy. But this is not sufficient; you must also observe the natural decay of the human body.

Now you are led to examine the cause and progress of this decay and forced to spend months in burial vaults and charnel houses. You see terrible things. You see how the fine form of man is degraded and wasted; you see how the worm inherits the wonders of the eye and brain. You examine the change from life to death, and death to life, until from the midst of this darkness a sudden light breaks in upon you—you succeed in discovering the cause of life; nay, more, you become capable of making lifeless matter come to life!

Turn to page 70

Suddenly it is clear to you what must happen. Suddenly you realize how you can raise yourself from this deep melancholy.

"Of course!" you exclaim.

From behind your door, you hear the voices of Elizabeth and Leon.

"Are you well, Father?" asks Leon. "It sounds as though something has disturbed you."

"Please let us know how we can help you," pleads Elizabeth.

"You can help me by standing out of my way," you tell them both as you throw open the door, brush them aside, and head down the hall.

"Where are you going?" screams Elizabeth. "Let us speak to you!"

You ignore their pleas, rushing into your laboratory. You quickly clear your worktables of all the equipment you had set up for the maintenance of Leon. It is time for a new project, one that will bring you great joy.

Elizabeth bounds into the laboratory breathless, hoping again that you will speak to her.

Before she can begin, you raise your finger to your lips to beg her to be silent. She acquiesces, and for a moment, you stand and study her every feature.

"Yes, the work I am about to undertake will require utter silence and deep concentration," you say. "But it also requires that I study you before you promise to leave me to my work."

You grab a piece of charcoal and a piece of paper and begin to sketch her face.

"Yes, this will be the hardest part to recreate," you say, "but that arduous task will be the most rewarding."

"Victor, what—"

"Shhhhhh," you say to Elizabeth. "I will hold you captive but one minute more, and then, dear cousin, I shall free you. You and Leon have my blessing."

You finish your sketch with a flourish, and then bow to her before retreating deeper into your laboratory. Now you are bent toward one task, and one task alone. If this Elizabeth will no longer have you, then you shall use all of your skills to create your own Elizabeth!

You labor day and night. Your goal is to recreate the perfection which nature had once succeeded in creating—

an Elizabeth, *your* Elizabeth. You know exactly what you wish, because you have seen it. Elizabeth is both your model and your muse.

You are surprised by how quickly you achieve your goal. Within a fortnight, you leave your laboratory with "Elizabeth" in tow. You find Elizabeth and Leon in the sitting room. They have been watching over you this whole time. You suddenly realize where all that food came from!

Your "Elizabeth" is still unsteady on her feet. You present her to Elizabeth and Leon.

Elizabeth gasps, and nearly falls to the ground. Leon holds her fast.

"Victor," she sighs, "do you mean to torture me? I cannot bear to look at myself. It is too disconcerting. It is as if I look in a mirror, and yet no mirror is here . . ."

Your new Elizabeth indeed looks like the original in every single way, except that she is larger, with a stature which matches Leon's.

"Elizabeth," you say, "I know it must give you an odd sensation to see yourself so, but I assure you she is nothing without your help. Yes, I need your help desperately to finish my creation, to breathe life into her. I know how to mold flesh into the likeness of another, yes, and for that I am grateful! Creating my lost love is the only way to heal my soul. But you . . ."

You look deep into her eyes, pleading with her.

". . . I need your tutelage once again. Please attend to her as you did with Leon. I am sure that after you are through with her, I will truly have you back. And then you, Leon, I, and, I hope, this new Elizabeth will be happy."

Though it is indeed a strange request, Elizabeth reluctantly agrees in the hope it will give you peace.

She spends the next month tutoring your new Elizabeth. Your cousin's gentle ways come into full bloom as she introduces your new creation to the overwhelming world and teaches her how to live within it. Her personality is truly transferred.

Most importantly, her love for you, for still love you she does, is also transferred into the new Elizabeth, and you soon marry, on the same day that your cousin marries Leon.

You forgive Elizabeth and Leon as your jealousy subsides, and your new Elizabeth becomes part of this strange family. You all become best friends, and you make amazing modifications to both of your creations. You find work teaching science at a university in Geneva, though you dare not impart your secrets upon your students.

You and Leon and the two Elizabeths live a long, beautiful life.

You continue to make modifications to Leon. His physical appearance becomes less monstrous. Elizabeth, your second creation, is much more fully formed. Aside from a few scars here and there, she looks exactly like the original design.

Leon has improved so much that fewer questions are asked by strangers. And even when questions are asked, thanks to the diligent work of Elizabeth, Leon can manage any argument, no matter how vitriolic.

In fact, he becomes so well liked by all, and so politic at discussion, that he ends up running for and becoming mayor of Geneva for a number of years after it becomes part of the Swiss Confederacy.

You have several children and grandchildren, as do Elizabeth and Leon. They are remarkably stronger than their peers, but by all accounts appear normal.

At the age of eighty-five, you succumb to a brief illness and die knowing that you made all the right decisions for this happy ending.

And when you pass away, the original Elizabeth follows shortly thereafter. The Elizabeth you created finds comfort in Leon, and your creations quietly spend another century together before finally growing old and dying in their simple cabin on the slopes of an Alpine village.

Though, as legend has it, that same Alpine village is today populated with the largest people ever seen . . .

THE END

You step back and throw down your galvanizing tool.

"You are right, friend," you say. You begin to weep. Your monster weeps with you.

"Be calm, my friend, it is all over now," says Clerval, patting your creation. He then turns to you. "You see, he has empathy. We can teach him!"

Under the cover of night, you bring your creation back to your apartment. From that moment on, Clerval moves in with you and helps you form the hulking mass of flesh into something more "human."

Turn to page 41

ou burst forth from your room and make a tearful proclamation:

"Though I am filled with sadness at your treacherous betrayals, I have decided that you need not suffer. Only I should suffer! Is this not my fault? Am I not the one who put everything in motion to create you?" You cannot say his name. "Was it not I who introduced you to Elizabeth? Nay, suffer not. You should live gloriously! And though I only look forward to a tortured existence, I will take solace in the fact that I did something for your happiness, Elizabeth. And for science! However, I shall never create another like him. I truly do wish you both the best."

You cannot bear to look at them any longer. You pack your things and leave them behind, never bothering to find out which paths their life together took. You stand by your promise to never create life again, though you put all you learned from creating Leon toward the betterment of science, and you become a noted chemist.

Henry Clerval pays you yearly visits. However, you never allow him to give you an update on your former fiancée and creation. In the autumn of your years, however, he comes bearing grave news.

"My dear Frankenstein," says he. "Elizabeth is gone."

Though you were less tortured by not witnessing their glorious life together, you now curse yourself for not at least relenting from time to time and checking on them. Deep down inside your very soul, you always loved Elizabeth.

At her funeral, you are reunited with Leon, who has made quite a name for himself as a gentle giant within Geneva business circles. He is a highly respected merchant.

"Father," says he, "it does me well to see you. It took every fiber of my being not to come to you through these many long seasons, though Clerval insisted I follow your wishes. Please join me now. Spend your remaining time with me. Let us tell stories to each other. What have you done with your life? Many glorious things, I am assured of that . . ."

Though you are still jealous that he spent a lifetime with your one true love, you remain with him. You tell each other wonderful stories. He gives you the utmost care as you grow old and die while he remains the same.

THE END

"*I* shall be with you on your wedding night!" Such is your sentence, and on that night the demon will destroy you, tear you from happiness, and plunge Elizabeth into despair. You cannot torture her so.

You return to your home in Geneva. Elizabeth welcomes you with warm affection, yet tears are in her eyes as she sees your thin frame and feverish cheeks.

Before she can speak, you embrace her and say, "I fear, my beloved girl, that I have seen and done things which have changed the very course of my life. My actions, though I may not divulge them, have led me away from you. You will always be to me as family, and I will always care for you, but we must not proceed with our wedding."

Elizabeth is devastated by your greeting. "Victor, have I waited this long only to be spurned by you? What have I done to deserve such a thing?"

You pull her closer to your bosom and assure her that

this is the best course of action for her, though you cannot say why.

Elizabeth declines into a great melancholy. Your father, too, whose final years were meant to be filled with peace, is beyond all consolation.

You can no longer share the same home with them, for they cannot accept your actions, and shun you. But you cannot live alone, for fear of losing your mind, filled only with memories of the terrible wrongs you have perpetrated. You have lost the only light in your life—Elizabeth—so that it may shine for others.

You fall into despair and wonder what you have left to live for if you are to be tortured so. You also wonder if the monster, who killed Clerval even after his promise to be with you on your wedding night, may kill again just to slake his thirst for revenge. You realize that your family will not be safe until either you or he has perished.

You journey once again to Montanvert, hoping to find your creation there. You beg for him to destroy you, your screams echoing among the crevasses of the massive glacier. Impassioned, your body out of control, you slip into an icy abyss and are no more.

THE END

Y ou turn on your galvanizing tool and rush at the hound.

"Die, demon dog!" you growl. "Die, or kill me in my attempt!!"

The hound evades you, but you reach the side of a cliff that not even it can scale. It teeters on the very edge as you jab the instrument into its flesh. The hound howls, but still does not relent. You push the tool farther, and a jolt of electricity tightens your hand around it. The hound flings the tool, and you along with it, down the face of the cliff. As you plummet, you look up to see the beast still wagging his tail. For the hound, all of this is merely a game.

Your body is found months later, and as a party leads you down to the base of the mountain, a howl frightens them. They rush down the mountain, never to speak of it again. Though when the wind is high on Mont Blanc, the mysterious howl can still be heard.

THE END

"**M**y dear father," you say. "It has been so long since I last saw you, and all I wish to do is embrace you and speak such words that would calm your mind and allow us to move on from the murder of William. However, I have news that must be spoken. This news is quite good for Justine. But it will doubtless plunge this family deeper into horror."

"My son," your father says. "Of what do you speak? Are you saying that Justine is innocent? But what evidence have you, and why is it so horrible?"

"In truth," you say, hesitating momentarily, "it is I who have murdered William!"

Your father swoons at this news. The gentle Elizabeth, who has just entered the room, holds him. You have not even had time to greet her properly, and she has now heard you are a murderer!

You help Elizabeth lay your father on a nearby chaise. You attempt to embrace her, but she steps back in horror.

Once he has recovered himself, your father says, "You? Murdered your own brother? Murdered our William?"

"Yes," you say, "though not by my own hand. You see, Father, shocking as it is . . ."

You tell your father and Elizabeth everything that transpired in Ingolstadt. He grows whiter with every new sentence as you reveal your gruesome secret that up until now you had kept locked deep within yourself. By the time you end, you feel a great weight is lifted off your shoulders.

Elizabeth breaks the silence that follows. "Dear cousin! I know not what to say. I know that your story is true. I never once doubted Justine's innocence, though am so saddened upon knowing the true murderer! For I can never look upon you again. Though I have waited these long days and nights for your return, I now wish nothing more than to be as far away from you as possible."

Elizabeth leaves the room. You throw yourself on the ground in front of your father.

"I beg of you, Father, do not shun me as my cousin has! Help me to find this creature and destroy him utterly."

Your father takes a moment to regain his composure, and then he looks at you and says, "Victor, I hereby swear to help you rid the earth of this creature. Though once it is done, you may never set foot in this broken house again."

You begin to protest, but he cuts you off with a wave of his hand. "My word is final! Though I lose a second son by exiling you, I can never look at you without thinking of your terrible deeds. I would last not a week in your presence! But I shall call upon the good citizens of Geneva. They will help us find this demon, and when we find him, we will indeed destroy him. However, the moment of his last breath shall also be the last moment I look upon you."

True to his word, your father rouses a group of men to action. You scour the countryside of Geneva, route out the fiend, and descend upon him in the dead of night with pitchforks and torches. The monster growls a terrible last breath. As he does so, your father looks away from you.

Shunned and detested by your countrymen, you return once again to Germany and eke out a meager existence as a physician to the poor. You feel that perhaps in assisting those of the lowest station you can make up for the terror to which you subjected your family.

You never see your father, Elizabeth, Ernest, or Henry again.

THE END

"I agree to your proposal," you say to von Hindenburg. "Relieve me of the monster I have created, and I promise to hone my scientific skills for the benefit of Prussia."

"Very well, then," says von Hindenburg. He rattles the gate, and a foot soldier appears to open it.

"See to it that Mr. Frankenstein's . . . friend . . . is dispatched at once," says von Hindenburg, and the foot soldier quickly turns and runs off to do the deed. Your heart sinks, a momentary lament for your first creation, but you know you have made the right decision. You know you can do much, much better.

"Tell me about this equipment of which you speak," you say to von Hindenburg.

"All in good time, Frankenstein," he replies, and puts his cap back on his head. "First, you must rest. There is much work ahead, and travel, too. I shall return to you in three days, at which point we shall head to an encampment near the front lines of the war with the French Republic. We will not have time for the leisurely pace of travel to which I am sure you are accustomed. You are one of us now . . . welcome to the Prussian Army, Doktor."

Before you can tell him you are not a doctor, von Hindenburg turns on his heel and leaves.

You take von Hindenburg's advice and rest. You sleep for a day and a half. Your feverish thoughts about what transpired on that fateful night—the night of the birth of your first creation—once again turn to exultation. The thought of returning to your endeavors energizes you.

By the third day, you lament that you know not where von Hindenburg is garrisoned in the city, for you would seek him out to implore him to begin the journey now.

To pass the time, you begin to meticulously clean and gather your tools—the tools of life! You lay them out in your apartment, and are just nearing the point of putting them in the appropriate cases, when there is a knock at your door.

Before you can even answer the door, von Hindenburg enters your apartment. He looks at the tools that you have laid out and quickly makes his first command. "Frankenstein," says he, "we have no time to pack such rudimentary tools. Take only what is necessary for your journey and let us be on our way."

You are much perturbed by the fact that von Hindenburg so quickly dismisses the tools you have spent countless hours molding into the bringers of life. However, you are eager to start this new phase of your scientific career, so you do not protest.

You pack lightly as requested, and von Hindenburg leads you to the carriage that awaits. He quickly shuffles you into the carriage and turns to leave.

"Will you not make the journey with me?" you ask him.

He makes a very clear answer by slamming the carriage door shut.

Turn to page 171

ou stare at the traveler, and there is something about them that makes you pity them. Yes, they are a monstrous sight. But looks can be deceiving. As a scientist, you know that just because someone looks like a monster does not mean they are a monster.

"I am sorry," you say, taking a breath as if to start over. "My studies can wait the extra hour or two it will take for us to find you shelter and something to eat. Of course. Please join us."

"Oh, thank you, sir!" cries the traveler.

You open the door and they come into the carriage. A sour odor enters with them, but you ignore it.

Again, as if reading your mind, the traveler says, "I apologize, but I have not bathed in weeks, and my diet has been so poor as to leave my breath with the sour odor of hunger."

"Do not worry," you say. "What is your name?"

"I am Karolina Weishaupt," she says.

"You are a woman?" you ask without thinking.

She does not seem offended, but sighs as she answers. "Yes, I am a woman. I was once someone's daughter, though my family have all abandoned me—or at least the person I appear to be. Now I am alone in this world."

The thought of a parent abandoning their child, even one with such a disfiguration, brings a deep melancholy into your heart. Karolina declines to say more. For many minutes, all that can be heard is the clomping of the beast's hooves.

Finally, you turn to query her further, but she holds up a hand and says, "No, no, I shall not burden you with my story. I assure you that it is even more horrific than my face. No, let us discuss your life. What is your name?"

"Victor Frankenstein, at your service," you say.

"And, young Frankenstein," she says, "to where do you journey?"

"I am bound for the University of Ingolstadt," you say, "to embark upon a study of science in the hopes of bettering mankind."

"Ah, I see," says Karolina. "You hope to better mankind, and yet, you almost left this poor woman on the side of the road." She chuckles.

A deep guilt fills your heart as you realize you nearly abandoned her merely to rush to your studies.

The carriage comes to a halt. In the darkness, you did not notice that you entered a small town some time ago. The driver stops in front of Schwarzhaus, and you head inside with Karolina.

The innkeeper is behind the bar, asleep. You gently wake him, but he starts when he sees Karolina standing next to you.

"What manner of creature is that?" he exclaims. "Do you intend to stop here for the night?"

"Indeed she does," you say. "And I would hope it is your intention to allow that."

The innkeeper looks from you to Karolina and says, "There are no vacancies. You should be able to reach the next inn before it closes if you hasten up the path with no delay."

"I know you are lying," you respond, "for why else would you still be behind the bar with no patrons at such a late hour? You are waiting to fill a room or two. This woman, though her appearance would indicate otherwise, is just as worthy as others to fill that room. I have the necessary money. To refuse would be inhuman."

He begrudgingly agrees, and you finally part ways with Karolina, bowing to her. "Thank you for teaching me something tonight."

"I know not what a poor wretch such as I could teach you," says Karolina, "but I shall say you are welcome."

You continue on your journey, and though many thoughts enter your head throughout, one remains constant. Until your art is honed to perfection, you cannot create a human from lifeless tissue, for anything so abhorrent would be turned away by humanity. Even something of nature—Karolina—could be so shunned.

When you arrive at the university, you can no longer bear to work with the horse leg you collected. You start with small creatures. You cut apart houseflies, sew them together with a fine thread, and bring them to life with the spark of your galvanizing tools—made of metal and charged with electricity from a generator you crank by hand.

Next, you reanimate frogs, swiftly emptying ponds of amphibians across the Bavarian countryside to collect your materials. The process is fraught with disappointment until you realize you must electrify the frogs within your claw-foot bathtub to keep them from drying out.

In the span of three months, you have not taken a single bath, but you have dozens of frogs in your apartment. They make quick work of eating your newly formed flies.

As bizarre as they are, you regard your frogs with pride. They growl instead of croak, dragging themselves about your apartment rather than hopping. One morning, you find several attached to your fingers, gnawing incessantly. They would have been successful at removing your digits if only they had teeth. They are indeed unnatural.

But you see in your first creations something special, a spark that could indeed ignite a conflagration.

The strength with which the frogs attacked the flies proves that the reanimation process imbues in them a greater fortitude than nature, you think.

You know it is time to expand your studies, to take another step, a bold step. You consider what to create next.

Perhaps a dog, you think. *Still small enough to control, but not so small that I couldn't learn something from the effort.*

The idea of a dog appeals to you. "Man's best friend," they call a hound—perhaps the very nature of a dog, that of a domesticated servant of man, would be the right next step in your growing army of creations. You believe you can train such an obedient creature!

At first, you doubt your decision to create a dog. It is hard to find fresh materials—dogs are not dissected in physiology classes in Ingolstadt, and as most carcasses of dead animals are treated like trash—not with respect, as with expired humans—good dog parts are hard to come by.

But once you put your mind to it, you are loathe to stop looking. You find a few small mutts that have expired in alleyways, though soon you resort to stealing older animals, the lapdogs of Ingolstadt's rich.

Still, these are not the optimal materials, and you realize that unless you come up with another idea, you may have to abandon your plan, unless you make a very small dog.

If you decide to make do with the materials at hand, turn to page 38

If you decide to think of another way to find dog parts, turn to page 108

"**E**NTER!" you yell. Your demon dog regards you but for a moment before the door opens.

You are shocked to see your good friend Henry Clerval enter the room.

"Frankenstein, I do not wish to disturb you if you labor, but . . ." Clerval's voice trails off. He regards the hound. The hound sniffs the air to learn more about Clerval.

You lie in shock, all plans to prepare a sedative frozen in your mind as you realize the unwitting bait behind the door is your best friend. Before you can yell at the hound, it pounces the full length of the room, knocking Clerval back.

"Henry!" you yell.

But it is too late. With a great cracking noise, the hound snaps Clerval's neck with its jaws. Your friend's body goes limp as life exits him swiftly.

"Nooooooooo!" you scream. You throw yourself at the demon dog. Not wishing to be disturbed while it feasts, it merely growls and carries off its newfound prey. You watch with horror as it springs down the steps and bursts through the front door into the courtyard as if it were constructed of paper.

You grab the deadliest galvanizing tool from your laboratory and rush down the stairs in pursuit. You look down to see a trail of blood. You follow the trail out of the courtyard and into the streets.

It is clear that the dog is attempting to remain unseen by humans, as the trail of blood travels through the least populated areas of town. The trail ends, and you know not where to turn. You stand breathless, spent from the effort of having to chase after the beast.

Just as you catch your breath, a scream pierces the quiet morning. The hound has not eluded all eyes. With a burst of fresh energy, you run toward the sound to find that a woman has fainted on the street. You rouse her and inquire whither the beast went.

The woman points, and you catch a glimpse of it up ahead, near where remnants of the old city wall block the ends of small alleyways. At the moment it reaches one of these alleyways, you let out a great yawp, and, frightened by the sound, the beast turns into it. You corner it there and pull out your galvanizing tool. It crackles ominously, echoing off the buildings along the alleyway.

Upon seeing you, the hound attempts to scale the old

city wall, but Clerval's body stops it from proceeding. You run up to jab the galvanizing instrument into its side. Before you can, the hound drops Clerval's body and leaps upon you. You drop down into the dirty alleyway together. The hound rears up and brings its jaws down toward you.

You roll to the right, and though the hound misses you, it tears into your coat. You jolt it with your instrument, but the fall has weakened its powers. The hound leaps back, but it is unharmed. It spits out a piece of your coat and leans menacingly over you.

But then it stops. It smells the air deeply like a hound attempting to track prey. Then it jumps over you and runs off. As much as it pains you, you must leave Clerval's mangled body in the alleyway in order to continue chasing the beast. You follow the sounds of screams south and out of town. But soon the screams are so far away you do not know where the hound is—only that it continues south.

You collapse in exhaustion, mourning your friend, and cursing yourself for creating such a beast. You wonder where it is headed, and suddenly you remember it smelling the air. You look down at your coat, torn asunder by the beast. This has been your coat since you were old enough to wear it, and your father's before that. Moreso than any other object, it reminds you of home.

Home . . . GENEVA! The beast flees in the exact direction of Geneva. What if it has caught the scent of your homeland?

For a beast with such strength and heightened senses, it may be possible.

You are dizzy at the thought of Elizabeth seeing such a creature or, worse still, being destroyed by it. You have to proceed home with great haste, but you know not if you have the strength.

Perhaps you would do well to alert the authorities. Indeed, the screams caused by the hound may have already done so. You could have assistance in capturing the beast. You need not tell them you created it; you can weave a tale about a rabid hound.

Still, if your idea of where the hound is headed is true, there is not much time. You may need to swiftly find transport south and hunt it down on your own.

If you alert the authorities,
turn to page 180

**If you hunt the hound down
on your own,** turn to page 86

*L*uckily, you have frogs to spare . . .

But the demon dog you have created is ravenous. It quickly finishes its meal of frogs and its attention turns toward you. You flee the laboratory, only to trip on the mess you have made of the parlor. You lie on your face, and you can hear the beast bounding behind you. You turn to see it bare its teeth with a great growl. Hot spittle flies from its lips.

Then, a knock on the door distracts you. Both you and the demon dog regard the door momentarily. You wonder from whom the knock came and assume the hound wonders what made the noise and how it tastes.

With the demon dog distracted, you attempt to slowly crawl away. But you move too quickly, and the dog is after you once again.

Then, another knock.

The hound licks his lips. A horrific realization cascades

through you. If you give whoever is behind the door permission to enter, the hound is bound to put all its efforts toward the newly arrived individual. It will be surprised, and it will pounce on its prey, that is for sure. That may be all the time you need to create a quick sedative and take away its willingness to fight.

But what if whoever is at the door is killed by this beast? you think.

If you take your chances with the hound, turn to page 84

If you give the person at the door permission to enter, turn to page 136

*L*ucky for you, von Hindenburg's offer is still valid. His men find your creature and destroy it. Upon its destruction, von Hindenburg wastes no time in utilizing your skills. He asks you to pack light, leave your equipment behind, and ride in the carriage he has arranged for you.

Turn to page 171

"I shall be with you on your wedding night!" Such is your sentence, and on that night the demon will destroy you and tear you from happiness. Well, be it so; a deadly struggle will then indeed take place, in which if he is victorious, you shall be at peace and his power over you will be at an end. If he is beaten, you shall be a free man. You resolve, therefore, to marry Elizabeth.

You return to your home in Geneva. Elizabeth welcomes you with warm affection, yet tears are in her eyes as she sees your thin frame and feverish cheeks. Her gentleness and soft looks of compassion make her a more fit companion for one as miserable as you are.

You embrace her and say, "Oh, Elizabeth, I cannot wait for the hour of our wedding and the peace—what little I may have—it shall bring. Still, I am haunted by one secret; when revealed to you, it will chill you with horror. I will reveal this tale of misery and terror to you the day after our marriage, for there must be perfect trust between us. But until then, I beg of you, do not mention it."

The tranquility which you now enjoy does not last. When you think of what has passed, a real insanity possesses you. Elizabeth alone has the power to draw you from these fits, her sweet voice returning you to reason.

As your marriage draws nearer, you feel your heart sink within you. You conceal your feelings by appearing happy. This brings joy to your father, but hardly deceives the ever-watchful Elizabeth.

Still, you must protect yourself from the fiend! You carry pistols and a dagger constantly and are ever on the watch. Indeed, as the wedding approaches, the threat appears more as a delusion, not worthy to disturb your peace. You begin to believe you may finally find happiness!

After the ceremony is performed, you commence your honeymoon journey to Villa Lavenza by water. The day is fair, the wind favorable; all smile on your departure.

You take the hand of Elizabeth. "Ah! The quiet and freedom from despair that this one day at least permits me to enjoy. But you are sorrowful, my love."

"Be happy, my dear Victor," replies Elizabeth. "There is, I hope, nothing to distress you. Though something whispers to me that all is not well, I will not listen to such a sinister voice. Regard the mountains and the water. What a divine day! How happy and serene all nature appears!"

When you land, you walk for a short time on the shore, enjoying the twilight, and then retire to the inn. Suddenly a heavy storm of rain descends. You had been calm during the day, but as soon as night obscures the shapes of objects, a thousand fears arise in your mind. You are anxious, and your right hand grasps a pistol which is hidden in your clothing; every sound terrifies you.

Trembling, Elizabeth asks, "What is it that bothers you, my dear Victor? What is it you fear?"

Her question brings a jolt of panic into your heart. What is it that you do fear? This whole time, you have assumed that you would be the target of his deathly promise! But what if he intends to bring harm to you by killing Elizabeth?

You know not whether to stay close to your love in order to protect her, or to send her to bed alone to keep her away if he should attack you and harm her if she remains.

What shall you do?

If you never leave Elizabeth's side, turn to page 93

If you stay in the living room when she goes to bed, turn to page 44

No, you shall not involve your dear cousin. However, you swiftly determine that you require assistance. You ask von Hindenburg to lend you a soldier, merely to move corpses and sort parts.

Despite the help, you have only managed to create five soldiers just hours before von Hindenburg's inspection. They regard you from the cages that von Hindenburg has fashioned for you as you attempt desperately to increase your efforts tenfold. The charnel house is too hot from your instruments, and the remaining bodies decay terribly. The odor is unbearable. You cannot move the bodies out, as they will freeze—winter has come early this year.

The moment of von Hindenburg's deadline has come. He arrives and regards the almost-empty cages in disbelief. Only five pairs of yellow eyes stare back at him.

"This is preposterous!" he bellows. "I asked for one hundred, and you give me five!! I merely hoped for twenty.

Even ten would have been acceptable. But five!? You insult me, Frankenstein!"

"I beg of you, Herr Kapitän, let me explain!" you plead, but von Hindenburg raises an eyebrow and a finger to silence you.

"You are a disgrace to the Prussian effort, and to science!" he says. He turns to the cages where your five monster soldiers are gathered. They have grown restless witnessing your argument.

"I shall set you free to see of what you are capable," says von Hindenburg. "We shall make use of you yet! And learn from his mistakes."

They quiver with excitement behind the cage doors, understanding he is about to set them free.

"No!" you scream. "I have not yet trained them!"

"They have no need of training," says von Hindenburg. "They merely have to be pointed in the right direction."

He swings the door violently open and points at you. "Destroy him!" he commands.

They descend upon you, like lions on a gazelle, tearing at your flesh.

You die.

THE END

"Very well," you say. "I shall make do."

"Very good, Herr Doktor," says von Hindenburg. "Very good. Three days! Be ready. I need one hundred more men."

But you know there is no chance for you to achieve what von Hindenburg requires. You and Igor decide to crudely reanimate all of your original creations and continue to sew on parts as the battle progresses.

When battle comes, the French forces once again overwhelm your legion of monsters. Using your sewing kit and your instruments of life, you revive the monster soldiers that are cut down by the enemy in the moment. You and Igor rush from corpse to corpse, and each soon turns into a soldier once again, but at a great cost. Each is wilder and more unbending to your will than ever before.

Yes, the monster army is getting more powerful, but if

you continue in this manner, you will soon lose control of your creations.

You know not how many times you must revive them in your efforts to hold back the French. You revive one monster that immediately turns on you. You plead with it to cease, but it kills a Prussian soldier near you. Soon, you are using your tools of life as tools of death to save yourself and Igor.

Now may be the time to stop this madness, though it means your certain death . . .

If you decide to throw down your tools on the battlefield and stop here, turn to page 11

If you create more and more monster soldiers, turn to page 164

"**N**o," you say dully. "There is no problem. Thank you for the . . . help."

Von Hindenburg lowers his eyebrow.

"Igor," says von Hindenburg, "this is the good Doktor Frankenstein. You will be working for him now."

"Good day," you say to Igor. You are not sure what else to say. This is all so bizarre. "It is a . . . pleasure to meet you."

"Now, Igor," von Hindenburg continues. "I must be clear about one thing. If you try to escape again, I will not be so lenient with you when it comes to punishment. This leather leash will seem like a beautiful necklace in comparison. I shall be in constant contact with your master about this."

Von Hindenburg motions toward you.

"Yes, Igor, you will act as if he is your master," von Hindenburg says. "You shall call him 'Master.' You shall do everything he tells you without fail. Doktor, you let me know if he does anything untoward."

You nod in agreement. With an assistant like this, you suddenly worry about the quality of the tools that shall be provided, though it is clear that you have no other choice.

Von Hindenburg tightens his gloves and straightens his hat. "Igor, you will take Doktor Frankenstein to see the materials and tools we have provided him, then begin by selecting the best meat to be used for his work. Doktor, we have gathered all the soldiers whose wounds were merely enough to kill them but not disfigure them greatly. Though I can tell you, we have much more to work with if you need it."

Von Hindenburg turns to leave with the soldier who brought Igor, but stops suddenly. He turns and raises a pointed finger in the air.

"Frankenstein," he says, "have no illusions. Your fate now lies with ours, so it would behoove you to do your best work as soon as possible. I need men. Strong men. One hundred. In a fortnight, when we advance. If we are overtaken by the French, I can assure you, you will be one of the first to die."

And with that, von Hindenburg disappears into the camp with his sergeant.

You turn to Igor. Who is this man? You are not sure what to say.

Igor says, "You must excuse my previous behavior. I assure you, it was merely my anger at being captured."

"From what were you trying to escape?" you ask, curious.

"From this wretched army," he continues. "I, like you, possess knowledge of science. I, too, wished to create life from death. However, where you have succeeded, I have failed. Before the Prussian Army found you, I was doomed to be executed for making a promise to von Hindenburg that I broke. I begged them to keep me as your assistant, assuring them that the task ahead was so great that you would need help. And you will indeed need help. But I never intended to help you. I always envisioned running away rather than facing someone whose talent was so much greater than mine. Sadly, I failed at that, too."

Igor looks in the direction where von Hindenburg marched and shudders.

"He is a man of his word," says Igor. "And sadly, now that you have made a promise, you must make good on your promise . . . or die."

Oh, how could you have been so weak as to get pulled into such dire circumstances? You swoon and nearly fall before Igor catches you.

"Thank you," you say.

"There is no need to thank me, Master," says Igor. "This

is now my role in life, and I fully accept it. I shall serve you until my dying breath!"

You stand up straight and regain your composure. You are indeed trapped, but all hope is not lost. You are now von Hindenburg's servant, just as Igor is yours. Inspired by Igor, you, too, determine to fulfill your duties.

"Very well, then," you say. "Take me to the tools."

"You shall be most pleased," Igor says. "Walk this way . . ."

Your fears soon melt away. The tools are beautiful, pristine, and perfectly suitable for the need. You gasp at the number of bodies set before you. All strong men, cut down in their prime, ready for your steady hands to be brought back to life.

So much better than creeping around graveyards, you think.

You are so filled with joy that you must fight the urge to embrace Igor.

"Very well, then," you say. "Help me sort the bodies downstairs, and then we shall set up our equipment in the tower."

Setting up your equipment in the tower proves to be a true stroke of genius. An early winter has brought forth a number of lightning bolts from a weather phenomenon known to the soldiers as *schneegewitter*: "thundersnow." Lightning strikes the iron tower and supercharges your equipment, so that you may work at a faster pace.

Igor proves himself to be most helpful. His methods greatly differ from yours, but you offer the proper guidance so that he may suitably assist you. You are grateful for his help—for, with his assistance, you do indeed create one hundred soldiers.

You have just begun their training—using torches to control them, for flame frightens them into submission—when von Hindenburg comes to inspect your ranks. He immediately goes to open the cages you have set them in.

"But, Herr Kapitän," you say, holding his hand still over the door bolt. "They have yet to be properly trained."

"Good Doktor," sneers von Hindenburg. "They merely need to be pointed in the right direction."

"No, I insist," you say.

Von Hindenburg slowly removes his hand from the bolt, though his countenance is one of great anger.

"I require at least a week to train them," you say. "This extra preparation will assure that I can add to their ranks, not replace them. They will defeat the French handily."

"Herr Doktor Frankenstein," von Hindenburg says, "I thought that you, as a man of knowledge, would understand that when I said I needed one hundred men in a fortnight, I also needed them trained. Regardless, I can see a brute strength in their massive forms. We shall march to the front line tomorrow. They shall join us in battle. As shall you and Igor. You must train them on the battlefield."

You have no choice but to remain silent, or risk the wrath of von Hindenburg.

Sadly, your prediction is correct. Your creations are ill-prepared for their battle with the French. Most of your time is spent keeping them from turning in the wrong direction. The French, in the throes of revolution, are stronger, sharper, and more committed to their goal than the Prussians. But you follow your legion of troops into battle, trying as hard as you can to will them to do your bidding. You watch in shock and horror as those you labored so intensely to create are dispatched quickly with large bayonets through the body.

As the Prussians retreat, you note which of your creations' brains would be of better use, those that were not shot in the head or dashed onto the ground. You note, too, which bodies have been run through, trying to assure the freshness of your materials for the next battle. Sadly, there is plenty of new material to work with as well—from both sides. You hope that von Hindenburg is not opposed to drafting French flesh into your ranks.

You dodge bullets to find the warmest livers and kidneys, passing them to Igor, who dutifully carries them off the field. You earmark the thickest skin with the fewest cuts. Through it all, you are saddened by the looks of fear on the faces of your creations.

You curse von Hindenburg. Once the battle has come to a gruesome end, you approach him.

"See?" you exclaim. "I told you that—"

Von Hindenburg raises a hand. "Never tell me what I should see or not see. I hope, Herr Doktor, that you were not about to tell me that I was wrong. I am never wrong. If your . . . monster army . . . is not ready for battle, that is your fault."

You force your anger away. "Begging your forgiveness, but it was agony to see my creations die in such a way on the battlefield."

"Yes," replies von Hindenburg in soft tones. "It is indeed terrible to see your men fall. However, at least you can revive yours."

"Well, not precisely," you say. "I believe I must start afresh. The first legion that I created needs so much work that—"

Again, von Hindenburg cuts you off. "We shall return to the battlefield in three nights. I highly suggest that you are ready."

"Three nights!?" you exclaim, raising your arms. "This is madness! We may as well throw raw meat at the enemy."

Von Hindenburg regards you with his steely eyes and growls, "Frankenstein, what do you think war is if not throwing raw meat at the enemy?"

You need more time—time von Hindenburg is unwilling to give you. You feel so strongly, you are not sure you can remain silent on this matter.

If you refuse to work with the time von Hindenburg has given you, turn to page 91

If you agree to revive your original monsters, turn to page 148

You cannot endure to mention the occurrences of the preceding night. You welcome your friend, therefore, in the most cordial manner, and you walk toward your university. Clerval continues talking for some time about your mutual friends and his own good fortune in being permitted to come to Ingolstadt.

"It gives me the greatest delight to see you," you say. "But tell me how you left my father, brothers, and Elizabeth."

"Very well, and very happy, only a little uneasy that they hear from you so seldom. But, my dear Frankenstein," he continues, stopping short and gazing full in your face, "I did not before remark how very ill you appear, so thin and pale; and you look as if you have been awake for several nights."

"You have guessed right; I have lately been so deeply engaged in one occupation that I have not allowed myself sufficient rest, but I sincerely hope that all my work is now at an end."

You walk with a quick pace, and you soon arrive at your university. You then reflect, and the thought makes you shiver, that the creature whom you created in your apartment might indeed have returned there, walking about and readying his revenge. You ask Clerval to remain a few minutes at the bottom of the stairs and dart up toward your room. You throw the door forcibly open . . . but nothing appears. The apartment is free from its hideous guest.

You yell down to Clerval to join you. When he enters your room, it is as if a great weight is suddenly off your shoulders. You swoon. You tremble and laugh nervously. You lose control of your body and flail your arms in despair.

"My dear Victor," cries he, "what, for God's sake, is the matter? How ill you are! What is the cause of all this?"

"Do not ask me," cry you, putting your hands before your eyes, for you think you see the dreaded monster glide into the room. "He can tell. Oh, save me! Save me!" You imagine that the monster seizes you; you struggle furiously and fall down in a fit.

This is the start of a nervous fever which confines you for several months. During all that time Henry is your only nurse. By very slow steps, you recover. It is a divine spring, and the season contributes greatly to your recovery. Your gloom disappears, and in a short time you become as cheerful as before you were attacked by the nervous fever.

"Dearest Clerval," you exclaim, "how very good you are to me."

"You will repay me entirely if you get well as fast as you can," says Clerval. "Others hope the same for you. In fact, you will perhaps be glad to see a letter that has been lying here some days for you; it is from your cousin, I believe."

You devour the letter from Elizabeth, who sends love to you through words, each of which you cherish. By the end of the letter, your heart swells only with joy and affection, and life seems completely back to normal. The wretched creature with which you imbued life has clearly moved on. If he were to have taken revenge, he would have already taken it.

You shun your own studies and dive into the studies that Henry has decided to pursue—languages of the lands that lie to Europe's east. After some time taking solace in your new studies, and your deepening friendship with Henry, you believe that the worst has passed.

You now look forward to returning to Geneva and your family. The month of May has commenced, and you expect the letter daily which will set the date of your departure, when Henry proposes a walking tour so you might bid farewell to the country you have so long inhabited. You pass a fortnight in these wanderings: Your health and spirits have long been restored, and they gain additional strength from the nature and the conversation of your friend. Excellent friend! How sincerely he does love you, and endeavors to bring peace to your mind. You become the same happy creature who, a few years ago, loved by all, had no sorrow or care. You are undisturbed by thoughts which during the preceding year pressed upon you.

On your return, you find a letter from your father. Your eyes scan it swiftly and regard a passage that puts a chill through your body:

"William is dead!—that sweet child, whose smiles delighted and warmed my heart! Victor, he is murdered!"

Your brother—dead! You throw the letter onto the table and cover your face with your hands. Clerval does his best to console you, and though you appreciate his counsel, you are so deep in mourning that you merely wish to return home as swiftly as possible. Clerval stays to continue his studies, and you travel alone.

You reach Geneva so late that the gates of the town are already shut. You resolve to visit the spot where your poor William was murdered. As you make your way there, a terrible storm breaks over your head. While you watch the storm, so beautiful yet terrific, you see in the gloom a figure behind a clump of trees near you. You stand fixed, gazing intently: you cannot be mistaken. A flash of lightning illuminates the object and instantly informs you that it is the wretch, the filthy demon, to whom you gave life. Why is he there? Could he be—you shudder at the thought—the murderer of your brother? As soon as that idea crosses your imagination, you become convinced of its truth; your teeth chatter, and you are forced to lean against a tree for support. The figure passes you quickly, and you lose it in the gloom. He is the murderer! You cannot doubt it. You think of pursuing the devil; but it would be in vain, for another flash shows him hanging among the rocks of the nearly perpendicular ascent of Mont Salêve. He soon reaches the summit and disappears.

Day dawns, and you hasten to your father's house. Your first thought is to instantly pursue the murderer. But you pause when you reflect on the story that you have to tell. A being whom you formed, and gave life, met you at midnight among the precipices of an inaccessible mountain. It would be regarded as the ravings of insanity. You resolve to remain silent.

You are shocked upon your arrival home to hear the news that the family servant, Justine, has been arrested and charged with William's murder. You cannot believe it. You know it was your creation that ended your younger brother's life!

Regardless, enough evidence was found upon Justine to lead the authorities to accuse her of the murder. And, poor confused girl, she acted in such a strange way upon being accused that the accusations stuck.

Though you *know* it in your soul that she did not murder

your brother, you fear speaking up to your father about this knowledge. What if he labels you a lunatic?

But you have created something that murdered your brother, and if it is found by the court that Justine is guilty, then two lives shall be lost.

What shall you do?

If you tell your father the truth to clear Justine's name, turn to page 124

If you continue to stay silent, turn to page 13

Y ou frantically continue to create monsters. You and Igor
are barely able to keep pace as they are struck down by
the French. Then the tide turns, and your powerful and angry
monsters defeat the French, guided away from destroying the
Prussians as well by the sheer willpower of you and Igor. You
wrangle them back into their cages and are able to take a
short break.

Von Hindenburg comes to inspect the ranks and tell you
that you move back to the battlefield tonight. However, when
you try to let a few out of their cages, they kill one of von
Hindeburg's sergeants in a fury. You and Igor force them
back into the cages, but they will be completely beyond your
control on the battlefield.

Von Hindenburg does not seem concerned. In fact, he
claims to have a plan for how to control your ragged monster
army.

"We know they dislike fire," he snarls. "So we shall use

torches to push them toward the French. They shall have no choice but to attack what is in their way to escape the lick of the flame."

You know it will not work. They will most likely turn on the people with the torches, their own soldiers, the Prussians. They already killed a handful of Prussians during the previous battle.

But rather than fight with von Hindenburg, you say, "That certainly sounds like it will work," and then come up with a plan of your own.

"Igor," you say, after von Hindenburg leaves. "There is only one way for me to stop what I have started."

"What is that, Master?" asks Igor.

"I . . . ," you hesitate. "I must become one of them!"

"What?" Igor stammers. "What . . . what are you saying!?"

"Igor," you say, "you must kill me. And then bring me back to life in the way that I have taught you."

"No, Master, no!" he exclaims. "The risk is too great! You shall not be able to control yourself."

"But it is the only way," you reply. "I must overcome them—and von Hindenburg—or die trying. You and I must be free of this. We must undo what we have done."

You argue passionately with Igor. You even threaten to kill him. He finally relents.

You lie on the slab. In a flash, he takes the life from

you with one of your galvanizing tools. There is nothing but darkness . . .

And in a flash, you come back! But everything has changed . . .

You suffer pain. Great pain. Your spine feels as though it is on fire. Your hands, clenched in agony, seek something to destroy, and thus quell your torment.

You cannot help yourself as you grab Igor and break his neck to relieve some of the agony that you suffer.

As you stomp over his lifeless body, you join the mass of monsters on their way to battle.

When von Hindenburg tries to push you toward the French, you, like your new friends, the only ones who know how you suffer, turn on the Prussians, crush them, and destroy them utterly.

You crush the French.

You lose yourself in your new body. Over time, you grow more powerful and less pained. But you have lost your mind.

Caught up in the madness, you tear through Europe with the wild pack of monsters, destroying villages and killing scores. In one large town, in the midst of the destruction, you see a familiar figure from afar.

Elizabeth? you think. *Elizabeth!*

For a moment, you remember who you are. You are Frankenstein.

But it is too late.

You have chosen your new life. You have chosen to be a terrible monster. You have chosen to survive.

You shall spare Elizabeth. Everyone else? You shall destroy them utterly.

THE END

You consent to listen to the tale of your odious companion. You eagerly seek a confirmation or denial that he murdered your innocent William. For the first time, also, you understand that you should make him happy before you complain of his wickedness.

He tells you how he learned to speak, by observing a family while hiding in a hovel near their home. Once sufficiently educated, he dared to speak with them. The father was blind and happy to have a visitor, but the others, upon seeing his unnatural form, ran from him. They fled their cottage, and he burnt it to the ground in a rage. With no safe refuge, he wandered the countryside. Every human he encountered turned him away, disgusted by his wretchedness.

So shunned was he by humanity that he tracked you down to have his revenge. He found you not, but came upon William, who said a Frankenstein was his father. Thinking he was your child, he strangled him and framed Justine for his death by putting the locket from round William's neck into her pocket as she slept.

"Thus ends my tale," says the monster, "and those shall be the last victims of my rage if you were to only comply with one request."

"What is it you request, monster?" you ask, terrified of his answer.

"I am alone and miserable, but one as deformed and horrible as myself would not shun me. You must create a female for me. This alone you can do, and I demand it of you as a right which you must not refuse, or else you shall curse the hour of your birth."

You are moved. You shudder when you think of the possible consequences of agreeing, but you feel that he is right. Do you not as his maker owe him all the happiness that is in your power to give?

He sees your mood change and continues swiftly, "If you agree, neither you nor any other human being shall ever see us again; I will go to the vast wilds of South America. I swear to you, by the earth which I inhabit, and by you that made me, my evil passions will flee, for I shall have the sympathy of another! But if you deny me, all I will have left is hatred and vice. The love of another will destroy the cause of my crimes!"

When you see the filthy mass that moves and talks, your

heart sickens. Still, you have no right to keep from him the small portion of happiness which is yet in your power to give.

Your heart is wrenched! You know not what to do! Aid this creature by giving him what he wishes, and you risk populating the earth with those like him. He swears to leave humanity in peace, but does he deceive you? Should you deceive him in return?

If you agree to his request,
turn to page 182

If you say you agree, but deceive him,
turn to page 75

Your journey is long and arduous. Several times, your driver, a soldier of the Prussian Army, has to jump off to clear the path of debris. Each time, you want to exit the carriage to assist, but the door is locked.

You begin to panic. *I am now a prisoner of the Prussian Army*, you think. You have no idea to where exactly you travel.

"Pardon me! Might you tell me our final destination?" you call to your driver, above the clatter of hooves. But he does not answer you, perhaps sworn to secrecy by von Hindenburg himself.

You journey for a full day and a half without stopping to rest. Old drivers are replaced by new ones. You are never let to exit the carriage, except to use the bathroom.

Finally, you arrive at a battlefield somewhere on the outskirts of the French Republic.

Upon your arrival, you are shocked to see the state of

things. It is chaos! The Prussians are ill-prepared for their conflict with France, which is undergoing a revolution. You pass earth scarred with cannon fire. You pass bodies mangled by bayonets. You pass tents. Haggard-looking soldiers are shuffling from one place to another, attempting to warm their bones in front of fires stoked with every fuel imaginable.

Finally, you can see von Hindenburg up ahead. Your driver stops the carriage and you alight.

You are tired and angered by your treatment. You momentarily forget your place and yell at von Hindenburg. "How dare you treat me like this? How do you expect me to work without sleep? Without equipment? Where on earth have you brought me?"

Von Hindenburg ignores your questions and says, "Welcome, Doktor Frankenstein. Welcome to your new laboratory." He waves his arm over the fields before you, as if presenting you with a gift.

"Doktor?" you say, still angry. "I am not yet a doctor. I have yet to finish my studies."

"You shall find, Frankenstein," von Hindenburg says, "that what I say here goes. If I say you are a doctor, a doctor you shall be. Consider your studies finished. Yet another gift I have given you!"

You pause for a moment. Though you are wary of von Hindenburg and his intentions, this is still an amazing opportunity indeed . . . and, now, a title to match! Of course! You have achieved more in the field of science than anyone at the University of Ingolstadt! You are much more deserving of your title than the heathens that have merely paid for their degree!

"Thank you, Kapitän," you say. "I am grateful." You bow deeply. "Now, where is this equipment of which you speak? I must be shown it immediately to determine if the quality is appropriate."

A demented howl rises into the air; the sound of pure torture.

"What manner of creature is that?" you ask.

"That is your assistant," von Hindenburg says. "And it is he who will answer all of your questions."

In the distance, you see a soldier approach. He drags a man whom he has bound to some length of leather, like a man would leash a wild hound. The man at the end of the leash struggles the whole way, kicking up dirt.

As they approach, the guttural howls grow louder. Von Hindenburg bends down to the thrashing figure. You are surprised by the power with which von Hindenburg picks up the bound man. He holds him in front of his face and screams, "Igor, compose yourself!"

Von Hindenburg throws Igor to the ground. Igor rears up, howls even louder, then falls on his hands and knees. You notice that he has a hump on his upper back.

Igor jumps up and runs at von Hindenburg, raising his hands as if to scratch von Hindenburg's eyes. The soldier who holds his leash pulls back just as the leash becomes taut, nearly snapping the madman's neck.

He lands at your feet, coughing and sputtering, holding his throat. It is red from the chafe of the leather. Your mind swims with the thought that this man is meant to assist you with your work. Can you really work with such a wretch?

"Is there a problem, Herr Doktor?" asks von Hindenburg.

If you decide that you do not wish to work with Igor, turn to page 27

If you decide to allow Igor to work with you, turn to page 150

"**E**lizabeth!" you exclaim joyfully. "Yes, she above all others is the most patient and caring person I have ever met. The way she cared for my dying mother, and then cared for those of us who mourned, is proof of it! Her soothing words will surely bring reason to his unformed mind! I shall write to her immediately!"

"Wait, Frankenstein," Clerval says. "Save your paper. Do not write. Send me as your envoy. I greatly desire a break and can pause my studies momentarily. It would be better for one of us to explain to Elizabeth in person what we ask of her; to better assure that she is up to the task, and, of course, to assure her secrecy."

"Excellent idea, friend," you say. "I often forget how abnormal the situation is within which we find ourselves."

"Within which you have placed us," Clerval corrects you.

"And it behooves us to explain it to her properly. Though

she is an understanding woman, it would be best to do as you say."

The following weekend, Clerval is ready for his journey to Geneva. You and your creation see him off as he enters his carriage.

"I shall see you soon," you say. "Send a letter ahead to let me know what to expect of Elizabeth, and if in fact she has agreed to our project. You must, of course, take all the time you need to rest. The creature and I shall be fine."

While the weeks pass, you double your efforts in teaching your creation language so that he may introduce himself to Elizabeth. Both you and he are in good spirits.

You tell your creation of the impending arrival of a new guest, a new friend, in fact the person who is most dear to you—Elizabeth. The day finally arrives, and it seems as though the creature, having heard all the wonderful things you have said about Elizabeth, is just as excited about meeting her as you are about seeing her again.

Upon entering your apartment, Elizabeth wraps you in a deep embrace, and you both tear up with happiness.

"Oh, my dear, dear cousin," Elizabeth says as she gently strokes your face. "These many long months, I have wilted as a flower in the cold air not having you near me. Clerval has told me all about your—"

But before she can continue speaking, your creation

pushes you brusquely aside and embraces her in the same way that she just embraced you, nearly choking her.

"You are quite strong," says Elizabeth. "Clerval gave me much warning of your countenance, good friend, and so therefore I am not frightened. Please, however, release me."

The creature lets Elizabeth go, and leans back to admire her with a smile.

"Pleasure to . . . ," the creature croaks in a raspy voice. "Muh . . . me . . . meeeee."

"Oh, dear creature," says Elizabeth. "I believe you mean 'meet you,' yes?"

Elizabeth helps you in exactly the way you and Clerval thought she would. Two weeks after her arrival, the creature's behavior has improved by leaps and bounds. Indeed, he is close to becoming a true gentleman.

One evening, to thank Elizabeth for all the work she has done, you stop studying how you may best improve upon your creature's physical appearance—a sizeable task which has kept you occupied all hours of late—to cook a dinner for her. You lay it lovingly upon the table and call her in.

"Oh, cousin," she says. "My dear, what is this?"

"My sweet darling," you say, "I merely wished to show you my appreciation for what you have done with my creation."

"Oh, it is my pleasure," says Elizabeth. "In fact, you may stop calling him 'your creation.' He and I have decided that his name is Leon."

"What?" you gasp. "You have named him? Without . . . why, why, that is wonderful. Please, have a seat."

"Oh, dear, dear cousin," she says. "I am sorry, but I did promise him that we would continue our lessons immediately."

You're flummoxed, but can only think to say, "Of course. Thank you."

She heads off to him, and you cannot help but quietly follow. What you see next makes your pulse quicken.

"Hello, my dear," says your creature—the one she has named "Leon."

"Oh, I thought I would never break away soon enough my darling," she says, and embraces him fully. "I hope my brief exit did not torment you . . ."

Before you can hear any more, you rush back to the dining room and, in a rage, flip over the table of food you had so delicately set out for Elizabeth. If you do not stop what is happening between Elizabeth and Leon, she may very well grow affections for him that eclipse her affections for you.

On the other hand, you are indeed quite proud of how far he has come.

What are you going to *do* about this?

If you put an end to their relationship, turn to page 78

If you allow things to proceed, turn to page 67

After a moment of contemplation, you realize you cannot hunt the hound alone. You head to the local magistrate's office. There, you report that your friend has been ravaged by a wild dog and left for dead in an alleyway.

Police officers accompany you to the alleyway. Upon seeing Henry dead, and altogether overwhelmed from countless sleepless nights, you weep in agony over Henry's body.

"What is the matter with you, man?" asks one police officer. "You appear unhinged."

"Pardon me, officers," you say, wiping away your tears. "I am merely overcome to see such a dear friend so soon taken from his life. I could not save him from the hound."

"You were here when this 'beast' attacked?" asks the second police officer. "Tell me what happened, step by step."

You relate more about the hound to the police officers.

You say not a word about your role in bringing the loathsome beast to life. But as you spin your tale, they begin to think you are telling a large lie. They believe that you are the one who has killed Henry Clerval.

You scream as you are dragged into a jail cell. They leave you in the jail for weeks, hoping you will confess. You go mad with the knowledge that the hound seeks your family.

Finally, you determine to tell them the whole truth. You relate the tale of how you created a hound of unimaginable strength and skill that is now set on a course to destroy your entire family. Although they do not believe this story, you are spared from the gallows. You end up in an insane asylum.

You are allowed to write your family, but any mention of the hound is crossed out of your letters by the staff of the insane asylum. You know because your family's replies make no note of it.

And soon there are no replies at all. You spiral into madness.

THE END

ou pause some time to reflect on all he has said. You conclude that, for the benefit of your creature and humanity, you should comply with his request.

"I agree to your demand," you say, "on your solemn oath to quit Europe—and all places where men may roam—forever, as soon as I deliver you a female who will accompany you in your exile."

"I swear," he cries, "by the sun, and by the blue sky of heaven, and by the fire of love that burns my heart, that if you grant my prayer, you shall never behold me again. Commence your labors; I shall watch your progress with unspeakable anxiety. When you are ready, I shall appear."

Saying this, he suddenly leaves you, fearful, perhaps, of any change in your feelings. After you see him descend the mountain with greater speed than the flight of an eagle, you slowly wind your way down the mountain. You wonder if he watches you even now. If he does, surely he can see the doubt forming on your face. You have set an abhorrent task for yourself, one which, when complete, will bring you peace, but which you dread more and more as you draw closer to your home.

Your wild appearance alarms your family upon your return. But you answer no question; barely do you speak. You feel as if never more might you enjoy companionship with them. But you love them; and to save them, you resolve to dedicate yourself to your most loathed task.

The days pass, and you do anything and everything to avoid the task set forth by your creation. You are sullen and forlorn, and your father, ever watchful, quickly notices. He questions if you have fallen into such a wretched state because you found someone other than Elizabeth that you wish to marry. In truth, you wish for nothing more in life than to be bound to Elizabeth forever—but when?

Suddenly, you are filled with a thought that both enlivens and terrifies you. What if you confide in the angel Elizabeth so that she may support you in your hour of terror? You could use her counsel to ensure that you create a woman who shall become the true companion to your first gruesome creation—one who would assure a perfect union. In addition, you would no longer have to live your entire life with the secret of what you have done. Your heart swells!

And then sinks, for how can you inflict such pain and mental anguish on *your* most beloved companion?

If you confide in Elizabeth,
turn to page 19

**If you decide to return to Elizabeth
after your gruesome task is finished,**
turn to page 96

The monster's face is the picture of malice and treachery. You think with a sensation of true madness on your promise of creating another like him and, trembling with passion, tear to pieces the thing on which you are working. The wretch sees you destroy the creature and, with a howl of devilish despair and revenge, disappears from the window.

You tremble from head to foot; you are overcome by the sensation of helplessness so often felt in frightful dreams, when you in vain wish to fly from a danger but are rooted to the spot.

The door opens, and the wretch whom you dread appears. Shutting the door, he approaches you and says in a smothered voice, "You have destroyed the work which you began! Do you dare to break your promise? Do you dare destroy my hopes?"

"Be gone! I do break my promise; never will I create

another like yourself, equal in deformity and wickedness."

"Remember that I have power; you believe yourself miserable, but I can make you so wretched that you will hate the light of day. You are my creator, but I am your master; obey!"

"I am sure of my decision, and your words will only increase my rage."

The monster sees the determination in your face and gnashes his teeth in anger. "Man! You may hate, but beware! You can destroy my other passions, but revenge remains—I may die, but first you shall curse the sun that gazes on your misery."

"Devil, cease; and do not poison the air with these sounds of hatred. Leave me."

"It is well. I go; but remember, I shall be with you on your wedding night."

You try to stop him, but he escapes and rushes from the house. In a few moments, you see him in his boat, which shoots across the water and is soon lost among the waves.

His words ring in your ears—"I shall be with you on your wedding night." In that hour you shall die. The idea does not move you to fear; yet when you think of your beloved Elizabeth's endless sorrow at finding your lifeless form, tears stream from your eyes. You resolve not to fall before your enemy without a bitter struggle.

It is your intention to flee this place and return to your loved ones. You take to the sea in a small ship to dispose of the parts used to make the devilish wretch's partner. When you return to your cabin, you scour the hut, removing all stains of your wretched wrongdoing, set it ablaze at sunrise, and return once again to the mainland.

You return to Perth to find solace in Clerval, only to find that not a soul knows where he is. You learn he left on a journey to your island. But your heart breaks, knowing that the monster, seeing your friend attempt to aid you, must have murdered him in revenge.

You spend countless days traveling south, but do not marvel at the cliffs of Dover as you pass them, do not take solace in the beauty of the Rhine Valley, note not the turns of river and road, only mourn those you have lost—and your future.

And what future have you? One of death! And so soon!

As you enter the gates of Geneva, perhaps for the last time in your tortured existence, a thought comes to you: You should not marry Elizabeth! Why torture her with a brief moment of peace, only to be followed by a lifetime of sorrow? Perhaps the monster will relent if he knows your soul is already tortured—and tortured it will be if you must spend your life without your love.

Still, you think, *perhaps I can overcome him. Am I not*

his creator? Who better to destroy him? Yes, you know his strengths, but you also know his weaknesses.

If you do not marry Elizabeth,
turn to page 121

If you proceed with the wedding,
turn to page 143